A VAMPIR T

C S

BELLA ROCCAFORTE

A novel set in A Vampire's Thirst World Created by A K Michaels ©

Disclaimer: This is a work of fiction. Names, characters, businesses, places, events, and incidents are either the product of the author's imagination or used in a fictional manner. Any resemblance of characters to actual persons, living or dead, is purely coincidental.

Notice: This is an adult erotic paranormal romance with love scenes and mature situations.
It is only intended for adult readers over the age of 18.

Cover design by: Monica La Porta. All stock purchased.

Chapter One

"Passion, lust, unrequited love." Grey unbuttons his black suit jacket as he paces across the front of his lecture hall. "That *undeniable* need to be near someone, have them, possess them, make them part of you..." He squeezes his eyes shut and balls his fist in front of him as though the passion of his words pain him in some way.

"*That* feeling is what a classic work of art is made of." A knowing smile stretches across Grey's full lips as he gazes out upon the swooning college students, hanging on his every word.

"Art is riddled with the twisted love affairs that we love to read, watch and learn about. They portray the fantasy of being swept off our feet and tangled in the throes of unbridled passion and lust."

Grey inhales a breath and watches to make sure his audience is still hooked, "The kind of passion that drives us to the ends of the Earth, deep into insanity to do whatever we must to please our lovers." He pauses, his expression darkens, "But the topic of love and art go hand in hand with pain, suffering and loss. This is why we will be studying the works featuring Persephone and Hades. A tragic love affair." He stops to study the moon-eyed students. A silent laugh rumbles within him, reveling in the folly of the living. Their youth brings on a nostalgia of a time when he was young, eager to love and he was alive.

"Their story is a legend that has been told for thousands of years through paintings, sculpture and written word. Why have artists found their story compelling enough to be inspired to action?" He waits for a response.

Melanie, the young woman who always sits in the front row of the lecture hall, turns in her homework early and always asks for a deeper understanding of the subject, inhales a breath moving tentatively in her seat. "Because Hades claimed Persephone, stole her away and then won her heart."

"That's one dimension." Grey nods flashing his stormy blue eyes in her direction. "But as we dig deeper into their story, we will find a myriad of delicate layers." Grey slides his pocket watch from his jacket and notes the time. "We're out of time for today, next week you have a paper due on the art and insight of why Hades and Persephone has compelled artists and remains a story that has been told through the ages. You will find all the requirements on the student portal online. You are dismissed."

As always the students linger, wanting to spend just one more moment with their dashing professor. Grey can smell their blood pumping hot through their veins, their pheromones oozing from their skin. He's no stranger to desire. He could have any one of them as a feeding host, a plaything or both. But he prides himself on the control he has developed over the centuries.

The students file out of the room slowly, but Melanie, as always, remains behind, "Professor Hart?"

"Yes, Melanie?" He says gathering his notes and placing them carefully in his briefcase.

"Why the story of Persephone and Hades?" She says fluttering her lashes.

Grey closes his briefcase and pins her with a look, "That's exactly the topic of your paper. I wouldn't want to take the fun out of it for you."

"I just wanted to get your insight. I'm very familiar with the story. I love Greek mythology." She leans both hands on his desk pushing her cleavage together to entice him, "It fascinates me."

"I'm glad you'll enjoy the subject then." He fastens the latches on his case. "I'll see you next week."

Dejected she turns and collects her things from her desk. "I'll see you next week, Professor Hart."

"Indeed." He doesn't look up at her.

He sniffs at the air and is immediately on alert. Dread fills him for a split second along with his need to protect Melanie from the vampire he smells nearby.

Grey blows out a reserved breath of relief when he sees a familiar vampire standing in the doorway.

Melanie smiles as she brushes by him, "Excuse me."

The vampire steps slightly out of her way, never taking his eyes off of her, "Certainly."

A sinister smile lights his features, and he begins to slow clap as he walks into the lecture hall, "Bravo, Grey."

"Charles." He acknowledges his oldest friend, his maker with a sense of foreboding. "What brings you to New York?"

"I just wanted to see if the master of control, was

still..." He sits in one of the desks and crosses one ankle over his leg, "In control."

"It's quite easy," Grey says moving around to the front of his desk.

"What I don't understand is, why?" Charles asks, genuinely curious. "You have all of this power, could have any or all of the women swooning over you in this classroom, yet you abstain?"

"I have found pleasure in so many other things, and prefer to avoid that type of distraction." He says leaning on the front of his desk. There's more to Grey's motives for control, but he keeps that close to his chest.

"I'm so glad to hear that," Charles says standing. "Let me buy you a drink."

Grey hesitates and rubs the stubble on his chin, "What do you want Charles?"

"That's why I like you, straight and to the point." Charles puts his arm around Grey leading him toward the door. "I have a proposal for you, we'll discuss it over dinner."

"I'm not particularly hungry," Grey says sliding

his case off the desk.

"You are tonight." Charles quirks his brow.

"I am not," Grey says stiffly. He'd rather get to the point, so he knows what awful task Charles has in store for him. "What is it you want, Charles."

"Fine. I would have preferred the niceties first. We could go to the hunting grounds, and you could indulge in some warm, live food for a change." Charles' eyes gleam with excitement awaiting Grey's response, hoping to hell he'll cave.

Grey swallows hard thinking of warm blood trickling down his throat. He feels the ticking of the pocket watch against his leg and is reminded of the destruction his loss of control can bring. "Now, Charles."

"That favor you owe me?" He pins Grey with a look that sends a shiver down his spine.

"I don't owe you a favor." Grey reminds Charles.

"Grey, you and I both know that you will always owe me a favor." Charles' voice deepens.

"What do you want." Grey grinds it out through his teeth.

"We have a problem, that someone with your control, and standing with The Directive," He pauses tugging at Grey's suit collar. "Is required."

"Please don't tell me I'm going on another fool's errand for The Directive." Grey rolls his eyes and starts out the door.

"Not a fool's errand, but a very delicate situation." Charles follows behind. "Where we'd like to save the life of a particular new vampire wreaking havoc in Atlanta. They must be stopped, immediately or they will be terminated."

"Did you make this vampire?" Grey's irritation grows knowing how irresponsible Charles has been in the past.

"It's possible, but I'm not sure." He answers quickly.

"And you need me to do your clean up." Grey shakes his head, "This is why I remain in control. So I don't have any 'delicate situations' of my own to deal with."

They step out of the building, dusk is taking over the Manhattan skyline as they get to the sidewalk and Grey hails a cab. They get into the back of the cab, Grey gives the driver his address, and he turns to Charles. "We'll talk more in a moment. Catch me up on what else you've been up to and how you've managed to escape Clarence's watchful eye."

"Clarence has been dealing with his own issues of late. I'm also no longer working with The Directive on a regular basis." He shrugs, "Just enough to know when I need to cover my ass."

"Or have *me* cover your ass." Grey shakes his head in frustration, "You know, there has to come a point when I no longer owe you a favor."

Charles' features begin to morph into the angry monstrous face of a vampire becoming enraged, "You will never stop owing your life to your father." He says with a growl.

The taxi driver glances in the rearview, his eyes flash with panic at the sight as his voice quivers. "Twelve dollars and sixty cents."

Grey swipes his card in the machine in the back seat and thanks the driver waving his hand, erasing the memory of Charles' face. "Thank you."

They get out of the cab and head into the luxury apartment building in Lower Manhattan. The doorman greets them with a smile. "So good to see you again Professor Hart."

"And also you Luis." Grey tips his head.

Once alone in the elevator, Grey turns to Charles, anger flashing in his eyes, "I never asked for this."

"What? Immortality, the ability to basically do whatever you want? Control humans at the wave of a hand." Charles blows out a breath, "Centuries have past, and you've still got that chip on your shoulder. Maybe if you learned to have a little fun you could --"

"Could what? Be running from The Directive because I overstepped the laws?" The doors to the elevator open and they step out together, "I've never created a vampire and won't. I will not take advantage of the innocent or those who are weaker than I. I'm not like you Charles, and you may be my father, but this is it. The last favor I will ever do for you."

"Wonderful." Charles smiles as he steps through the doorway of the apartment.

"What am I cleaning up?" Grey places his briefcase on the antique credenza.

"He's a sweet kid, but I may have misjudged things a bit," Charles says with a devil-may-care attitude that gets under Grey's skin.

"Misjudged things?" Grey's voice reaches an upper register.

"Well, it would seem that he's taken it upon himself to feed openly." Charles shrugs his shoulders.

"What do you want me to do? You're his father, you handle this mess." Grey goes to the wet bar and pours himself a scotch. He specifically doesn't offer one to Charles, which goes against his grain, but he's too angry for hospitality.

"I can't, the local office of The Directive is already sniffing around. I need to stay clear. But if you have to kill him, do it."

"Kill him?" Grey protests and downs his scotch

instead of sipping it. "If that's one of your options, why didn't you do it?"

"As it would happen, he's the son of a senator or governor or something like that. I really don't want to kill, since I'll be able to use him later, but you know I have no patience for newborns." Charles says it as though he's just asked Grey to take out the trash.

"I will not." Grey says with vehemence, "It's been centuries since I've taken a life."

"That's not true, World War One, Two? Or have you forgotten that?" Charles begins to lose himself in a memory, "Those were the days, feeding in the battlefield was...glorious."

"That doesn't count." A pang of guilt shoots through Grey at the thought, and the ticking of the watch feels louder momentarily in his pocket. "That was war."

"That was a smorgasbord." Charles smiles. "Much better than the plague, wouldn't you agree?"

Grey blows out a breath, "No, neither were pleasant."

"You're such a curmudgeon." Charles waves his

hand and pours himself a bourbon from the bar. "Let's order in." Charles picks up his phone. "All this talk of the good ole' days is making me hungry."

"I have blood, I will not have you feeding on a live donor in my home." Grey insists.

"Fine." Charles' shoulders slump in disappointment. "You will go to Atlanta, find Michael and you *will* take care of the problem." Charles awaits Grey's agreement.

"This is the last time," Grey says heading toward his bedroom. "I have to pack."

"Wonderful. When you get there, I will have Angus assist you."

"Angus?" Grey bristles at the mention of his name. "Why doesn't he handle this?" Grey asks annoyed.

"He's a brownie, he's not equipped, but he can help you find the vamp. Or anything else you desire while you're there. He's quite resourceful."

"I like him okay, I just don't prefer his...tactics." Disdain drips from Grey's tone.

"Exactly!" Charles lifts his finger, "And that's why I need someone that can exercise your level of control and practice discretion."

Grey blows out a frustrated breath. He knows he can't say no, if only for the newborn vampire lost in the city.

"And think of it this way, The Directive will be in your debt for solving this problem, so they don't have to." Charles points out. "You don't want poor Michael's first run-in with other supernaturals to be...unpleasant."

"Or deadly." Grey finishes.

"Yes, you know how The Directive loves when we clean up our own messes before they become disasters."

Chapter Two

The twinkling Atlanta skyline comes into view, Grey turns the headlights on and lowers his speed to something more reasonable. Throughout the centuries he's always enjoyed the speed afforded by being a vampire. His reflexes lightning fast and ability to see in the dark gives him the luxury of flying down highways as fast as his Bentley will carry him.

A crooked smirk cuts into his cheek remembering how just a short century ago this journey would have taken him two days on foot. Now, he can make the journey by car in less than six hours, depending on traffic.

He rolls into the valet at the Georgian Terrace Hotel, leaves the keys in the ignition and steps out of the car.

"Professor Hart, it's a pleasure to have you staying with us again." An older gentleman approaches the driver's side of the car.

"Thank you, William, it's a pleasure to be here." Grey smile's kindly. "Bags are in the back."

Grey adjusts his suit and continues to the concierge, "Good morning, Beatrice."

"Professor Hart, I was delighted to see your reservation this morning." The older woman clicks on the keyboard, her expression falls slightly. "There is a problem though."

"Yes?"

"Penthouse Four has been reserved for tomorrow." She says looking up at him with remorse.

"Is Penthouse Six available?" He asks.

"It is." She smiles.

"That will do then, you know how I love the balconies." Grey isn't above using his powers of persuasion, though he typically doesn't like to.

"Wonderful, I'll have William bring your bags up. Complimentary breakfast?" She says stopping typing.

"Not today. But thank you." He says taking the keycard and tapping it on the desk. "And please alert the staff of my usual accommodations."

"No maid service and you are not to be disturbed." She confirms.

"Yes, Beatrice, thank you." He heads for the elevator sliding the pocket watch from his jacket and checks the time. Six thirty AM. Hopefully, Angus is awake and ready to go. *I'd like to be home by Monday.* He thinks while pushing the button on the elevator.

When he gets to the room, he mashes the buttons on his cell phone to call Angus. The call goes straight to voicemail. He puts the phone back in his breast pocket of his suit jacket and steps out onto the balcony.

He revels in watching the city come to life in the morning hours. This is why he stays at the Georgian, it's one of the only hotels with balconies, and he remembers the grand opening in Nineteen Eleven. He remarks to himself how the city has changed, this used to be one of the tallest buildings, now it barely peeks over the next city block.

He inhales deeply and catches the scent of something luscious and alluring. He walks to the end of the balcony to get closer to where the scent is coming from. He inhales deeply again, and hunger stirs in the pit of his core. His stomach growls and churns in a way he hasn't felt in centuries and his cock ticks to life with the need to be touched. He's brought a small store of blood, which William should be delivering in his bags any moment.

He looks down on the street where there are a few pedestrians, the smell of their fresh warm blood entices him, he wants to jump down and feed on one of them.

The click-clack of a woman's heels rings in his head as he stalks her with his eyes, her tight skirt hugging her ass. He wants to bury his fangs and cock into her all at once. Drink from her as she wraps her bright red lips around his cock.

The sound of the elevator door opening momentarily snaps Grey out of his dark thoughts. He goes to the door opening it before William can knock.

William is taken aback when the door opens, "Professor Hart." He grasps his chest, "I really hate when you do that."

"Sorry, William. I'm just eager to get started on some work, and I need my bags." Grey apologizes, but his eyes are focused on the black bag carrying his blood.

"I understand." William rolls the cart into the foyer of the suite and unloads the bags. "Would you like me to put them in the bedroom?"

"No." Grey snaps, immediately feeling remorse for his behavior. "I'm so sorry. It was a long drive."

"Not a problem Professor Hart," William says

placing the bags on the floor quickly. William backs slowly toward the door rolling the cart with a sense of fear running through him.

Grey feels terrible, William is one of the good guys, he never asks questions and has been a bellman here for forty years.

"William, again I apologize." Grey hands him a folded up hundred dollar bill.

"No need for apologies professor Hart, thank you." William hesitantly takes the cash. "Let me know if you need anything."

"Will do," Grey says with a heavy sense of remorse, that is quickly replaced by the need to get to his food.

The door clicks closed, and Grey frantically digs into his bag of blood. He pours it into one of the wine glasses at the wet bar. He tries to sip the thick liquid slowly but gulps it down.

It's cold, lifeless running down his throat and nausea threatens at the edge of his control. He looks at the glass as though it has wronged him.

"Ugh, this is rubbish." He checks the bag of blood

to see when it was collected. It's only a few days old, typically fine for his enjoyment and satiating his hunger. But today, it just won't do.

The doorbell rings and Grey stomps to the door swinging it open, "What?"

Grey's eyes devour the young woman in a maid's uniform, her beating heart rings in his ears, it's all he can hear.

"I'm terribly sorry to disturb you, Mr. Hart, but the room has not been stocked." She looks down at the floor as she speaks to him.

"What fool didn't have the room ready?" He half bellows and then checks himself. "I'm so sorry, it was a very long drive, I don't know what's come over me. Please come in..." He checks her name tag. "Julia."

Julia's gaze remains down-turned as she enters the room with her cart. "Again, I apologize Mr. Hart."

Something dark and dangerous in Grey takes over, and more than just his hunger for blood is stirring. Her feminine scent arouses parts of him that he's had control of for centuries. But he needs her. He wants her. He's going to take her.

She begins to unload beverages and snacks from the cart and glances up at him getting lost in his good looks. Her pheromones go wild, and the scent of warm pussy fills Grey's senses.

Grey takes the snacks from her hands setting them on the counter. "Call me Grey."

She stills, gazing into his eyes. "Yes, sir." She's lost in them, a clear blue that she could swim in for days.

Grey wraps his arms around her, sniffing her hair, "I said call me Grey."

"Yes Grey," She says reveling in the strength of his embrace as he runs his lips close to her neck.

Grey can smell her arousal matches his own. His cock springs to life, he has to have her, but he must ask permission, "Julia," He says in a sultry voice, careful not to use his power of persuasion.

"Yes." It comes out on a baited whisper.

"I want you." He growls in her ear.

She looks up at him through hooded lashes, her

fingers digging into his solid biceps. "I want you too."

Grey runs his hands down her back until they're firmly planted on her ass. He hikes her up, and she wraps her legs around him. He carries her to the couch and sets her down pushing her dress up catching sight of her thigh high stockings his eyes flick to hers, "Naughty girl."

Her cheeks flush red as her answer, she runs her fingers through his hair and pulls his lips to hers.

Her warmth against him drives him wild with more desire than he can handle. His tongue dances in her mouth and his fingers travel to her most sensitive parts. He pushes her panties aside and feels the moisture at her core. His fingers slide effortlessly inside her, and she moans with pleasure.

"Grey." She sputters, and he stops for a moment.

"Is this okay? Would you like me to continue?" He's trying to remain in control of his desire, but can't. He needs her to say yes.

"Yes, please don't stop." She begs throwing her head back with pleasure.

He continues working his fingers inside her and

runs his tongue along her neck, her jugular taunting him pumping blood hot and wild. He wants to sink his fangs into her and drink, satiate his parched throat. He holds back, just nibbling and teasing, but unsure how long he'll be able to control his thirst.

He slides her dress down to the floor, dragging his lips across her breasts. It's been so long since he's felt the warmth of a human and he loses himself in the feeling. He teases her hardened nipples rolling them between his thumb and forefinger. He works his way down between her thighs, teasing and taunting.

Julia releases an uneven gasp in ecstasy with a primal moan, "Oh God."

The sound of her femoral artery pounding in Grey's ears is deafening. He needs to drink from her in all ways, his tongue dances and plays on her thigh before he flicks a glance up between her legs exposing his fangs. "May I?'

Julia nods and lets out a breathy "Yes. Drink from me."

His fangs pierce effortlessly through her supple skin. Warm, thick liquid fills his mouth with an incredible sensation of pleasure. He drinks from her, while his fingers still work inside her finding the sensitive bundle of nerves. The walls of her pussy contract around his fingers signaling her first orgasm ripping screams of pleasure from her core.

Grey's cock demands attention, he stands dropping his pants to the ground and lifts her up taking her to the bedroom. Grey hovers over her, ready to plunge into her. The sweet taste of her blood still burning hot in his mouth, he licks the fingers that were inside her. He glares at her with undeniable lust as he licks the last of her essence from his finger, "Delicious."

She pants and bites her lower lip as she tries to recover from her climax.

Grey lifts her ass to meet him, her soft warm, walls surround his rock hard cock, he takes a moment to savor the sensation.

Julia lets out a low growl, "Fuck me."

"I intend to." Grey responds moving in and out of her, "Tell me how you like it."

"Hard, fast, just fuck me." She grits out, begging him for more.

He flips her over on the bed propping her ass in the air. He leans down and flicks his tongue over her already swollen clit. She rewards him with another squeal of pleasure.

He strokes her wet pussy with his fingers before sliding his shaft inside her again. He thrusts deep into her while rolling her clit with his fingers, applying just the right amount of pressure. "You like that?" He growls wanting to fuck her harder.

"Yes, oh God yes. More, give me more." She shrieks whipping her head around wildly.

The sheets ball up in her gripping fingers. Julia's trying to hold on, her climax comes hard and fast. Her movements are out of control, her toes curl as Grey releases inside her. She rattles off a string of expletives unable to control her convulsions or her voice.

Julia lowers herself face down on the bed barely able to catch her breath.

Grey wipes the sweat from his brow and slaps her playfully on the ass, "Again?"

Julia rolls over pinning him with a lustful yearning, "Yes."

He climbs up moving his tongue up her form. He tangles his hands in her hair, moving her head to explode her jugular, "May I, again?"

Julia threads her hands behind Grey's neck, digs her nails in and raises her hips rubbing her clit against his cock, "You give me that, and you can have whatever you want."

Grey sinks his fangs into her vein and plunges his cock into her welcoming cleft. Julia reacts with a wild growl, "Fuck yes."

He pounds her hole as she continues to respond to him, her walls convulsing around him, her blood flowing into his mouth.

"Whoa!" Angus appears in the room, yelling out. "Grey, you need to stop."

Grey ignores the annoying red-headed

Brownie continuing to drink from Julia. He feels her life force ebbing, and he wants all of it.

"She's going to die!" Angus' voice reaches an upper register as he takes the risk of trying to pull Grey off of her.

Grey shakes Angus'' hands from his shoulders and pauses for a moment, his mouth agape staring at Julia. He scrambles off of her, instantly disgusted with himself.

Her skin is pale as she moves lethargically turning her head to look him in the eye, "Take what you need."

Grey quickly scoots backward on the bed. Reality sinking in at how close he was too draining her completely. He drags his fingers through his hair shaking his head, "Shit."

"Shit is right." Angus appears beside the bed holding a glass of orange juice and a bag of snacks from Julia's cart. He urges Julia to sit up, "Here you go lass, drink, you'll feel better."

Julia sluggishly sits up taking a drink from the

glass. After a few sips, she pulls the sheets up to her neck. "What happened?"

Angus releases a nervous laugh, "You two got a little carried away, but all is well. Eat this and take a rest, you'll be fine in a bit." His Irish brogue goes a long way to soothe her immediate panic.

Grey turns back toward, "Sorry, love, it's been awhile."

Her eyes gloss over with lust, "It's okay, I enjoyed every minute of it."

Angus places the bag of snacks in Julia's lap and the juice on the bedside table. He turns to Grey, ticking his head toward the living room of the suite. "A moment?"

Grey turns back to Julia, "I'll be back shortly."

He leaves for the living room, finds his trousers and pulls them up leaving the belt undone. Regret and satisfaction battle inside him for dominance. He wants more, he needs more, but his conscience is creeping in.

"What the hell were you thinking?" Angus asks him wide-eyed.

"I don't know..." Grey stammers pacing the floor.

"You were sent here to stop this kind of madness, not be part of it." Angus takes a risky stance with the ancient vampire. But his anger at the prospect of yet another clean up is ruling. "I finally get rid of Charles, in hopes of keeping The Directive out of here just to have you coming down here and making it worse?"

Angus shakes his head wringing his hands, "A hotel maid? Have you gone mad?"

"I'm sorry Angus, I-I-I don't know what's come over me." Grey searches his memory for some kind of trigger, anything that made him lose his control.

"I've known you a long time, never have I seen you like this. When did you start feeding from live donors again? You've been off that for ages!" Angus scolds.

"Today." Grey breathes the words, a flash of the memory of his last live feeding shoots through his mind.

"Well, you picked a fine day to fall off the wagon." Angus plops down hard in the chair exasperated.

"What are you going to do?"

"She won't remember, I'll see to that." Grey glances toward the bedroom door.

"You'd better, and be in a hurry, we've got work to do." Angus checks his watch. "I know where Michael is now, but as soon as the sun sets, he'll be on the move."

"Michael?" Grey questions.

"The reason you're here? Another one of Charles' bastard children?" He pulls his lips to the side, "Vampires...I need a new line of work."

"Oh yes, Michael. So sorry." Grey struggles to shed the confusion of his Thirst pulsing inside him. He can hear Julia's blood flowing stronger in her veins, and he wants it. Another sound in the hallway draws his attention right before the doorbell to the suite rings.

"Bloody hell." Angus looks at the door with a mask of alarm.

"I got it." Grey goes to the door. "Can I help you?"

"Professor Hart." An older woman with a scowl is standing in the hallway. Her expression immediately lightens at seeing Grey's bare chest. Her eyebrow quirks involuntarily.

"Yes." He says trying not to sound impatient.

"Is everything to your satisfaction?" She asks.

A lewd smile dances on his lips, "Yes, everything is wonderful."

"Excellent, I did, however, want to apologize for the suite not being fully stocked when you arrived." Her eyes drag down his body.

"It's quite alright," Grey's steps back into the suite, "It's all taken care of now."

"Wonderful," She turns from the door and stops, "Oh, also, have you seen Julia since this morning? She's not answering her pages."

"Yes actually." Grey's mind races at what to say, how to keep Julia from being reprimanded. He sets his stance in the doorway. "As it would happen there were several things out of order in the suite, Julia has been here correcting the issues."

"Oh really?" The woman says full of concern.

Grey waves his hand to persuade her thoughts, "She's a wonderful asset to your staff. She should be recognized for her excellence."

"Of course Professor Hart. I will be sure to note her file. I'm glad she has been able to take care of the 'issues'." She says.

"Yes, and thank you." He looks deeply into her eyes, "Now, continue about your business."

"I'll be continuing about my business." She walks toward the elevator with a slight spring in her step.

Grey closes the door and releases a strained breath. Angus has a look of admiration, "When did you learn to do that?"

"Do what?" Grey asks going to the bar to pour himself a scotch.

"The whole 'continue about your business' bit." Angus bellies up to the bar expectantly.

"I've always been able to do it, I prefer not to." Grey looks toward the bedroom door nervously. He can hear Julia's heart pumping stronger again, almost back to normal.

"Do you also have the power to make her forget?" Angus asks.

"Thankfully, yes."

A Vampire's Thirst

Chapter Three

Grey grips the arms of the chair as Julia puts the last of the used towels on her cart. He watches, listening to the sound of her blood flowing through her. He wants more, needs more.

Angus positions himself between Grey and Julia, knowing that Grey's about to lose it again. "Thank ya, lass. We appreciate you."

"It's my pleasure." She looks past Angus, "Again Professor Hart, I'm so sorry the room was not ready."

"Not to worry Julia. Thank you." Grey fights the urge to get up. First to be a gentleman and open the door for her, second to taste her again, all of her. He breathes a sigh of relief when the door clicks closed.

Angus spins around, "Okay, let's get moving. It's going to be dark soon, and Michael will be on the move."

Grey stills himself before getting up, "Yes, let's get this over with. I would like to be home by Monday."

The thought of leaving sets something off inside him, it causes him pain. He must stay nearby. He's always enjoyed Atlanta, but never enough to live here, only to visit. Yet he feels as though he couldn't bring himself to leave.

"Grey. Are you listening to me?" Angus snaps Grey out of his trance.

"Yes, sorry. What?" He asks.

"We're going to the Bubblegum Factory," Angus says.

"Where's that?" Grey recalls the name but has

never been there. That's not his type of place.

"It's down on Cheshire Bridge Road, stripper's row." Angus delights in the thought of being in the seedier part of town.

"Why?" Grey asks annoyed.

"Strip clubs, perfect for vamps. They're open twenty-four hours and no windows." Angus nods once as though it was his very own idea.

"Wonderful." Grey stands straightening his suit. "Have you alerted the Atlanta Company?"

"We haven't had an issue like this in a long time. I'm not really sure, and aside from you, I prefer not to spend too much time with Vamps." Angus says pulling collar a little higher on his neck.

"I understand, I prefer to avoid my own kind." Grey remarks heading for the door. "Let's get this done and please find out if the Atlanta Company is prepared for a new 'patient'. I really don't want to bring this baby back to New York to train him. I've been down that road with Charles' messes before."

Grey grips the steering wheel. Fever, desire and thirst pound at his control. So many delightful flavors fill the air. He needs to let loose. He needs to feed. The intoxicating scent from earlier still dances in the air, luring him to let loose.

"You okay there?" Angus asks holding tight in his seat.

"I'm fine." Grey grinds out through his teeth. "Where is the closest feeding ground?"

Angus is taken aback, "You just fed."

Grey growls at him, "Yes, and I will feed again soon, even if it's from you."

The blood drains from Angus' face, "Grey, you have to get hold of yourself. This isn't like you."

Grey yanks at the steering wheel pulling into the parking lot of a strip club. He gets out of the car leaving it running and the door open.

Angus sits stunned for a moment before grabbing

the keys and going after Grey, "Hey, hold on. What are we doing here, this isn't the club Michael's at."

Grey doesn't answer, he pays his money at the door and stalks inside. He scans the room looking for the sweet scent that drew him here. It's something he's never sensed before. Delightful, intoxicating and he has to find it.

Angus comes to a stop behind him, "We really need to get to Michael before he's on the move."

Grey snaps out of his trance. A look of disgust crosses his features. He lets out a groan at the unsavory lot populating the dirty strip club.

"That's a good vampire. You'd never feed on these low lifes." Angus' shoulders relax at seeing Grey looking more lucid. Angus tugs at Grey's jacket, "Let's get to the Bubblegum Factory."

Grey shakes him off sniffing at the air, "There it is again." He moves forward with purpose toward the back room.

He bursts through the door, the room is empty but for the tables and chairs. There's a cigarette still smoking in the ashtray and a half drunk glass of wine. He picks up the glass of wine studying the lip print on the rim.

"Grey, there's no one here, let's get on with this." Angus prods him.

Grey looks up at him with disdain, he wants to rip his vocal chords out to shut him up. His fist is balled at his side trying to control his rage. He's about to do it, to shut him up.

Two women wearing next to nothing come up behind Angus. Grey loosens his shoulders at the sight and smell of them. He's thirsty in more ways than one.

"Hello, handsome." One of them says pushing past Angus.

"Hello, ladies," Grey says with a charming smile.

"Can we get you anything?" The redhead comes to a stop directly in front of Grey and runs her fingers under his collar.

"I think you can." A lascivious look crosses his features as he grabs a handful of her ass.

"What's your pleasure?" The blonde asks from the doorway.

"I'll have a Scotch to start." Grey doesn't take his eyes off the redhead. "What is your name?"

"I'm Ruby." She says rubbing up against the erection growing his pants.

"Of course you are." Angus blurts out. "Grey, we don't have time for this."

"There's always time for pleasure." Grey is rock hard and ready. Images of fucking and drinking Ruby run through his mind. He takes her, pressing his lips against hers hard and forceful.

She loves it, she wants him, there's no resistance, and she reciprocates allowing him to enter her mouth.

"Oh for the love of God," Angus cringes, "Grey, these girls don't have sex. They're for show only." He tugs at Grey's jacket.

"Not this girl," Ruby says in a hungry breath.

"Oh, that's even worse." Angus groans, "You kissed her on the mouth."

"Shut up, Angus." Grey turns to him.

"Grey, come on. We've got to get out of here." Angus pleads with him.

Grey can't resist the sound of blood pumping through her veins. He has to drink. Without asking permission, he sinks his teeth into her neck and drinks from her. Ruby's eyes roll back in her head with the ecstasy of the sensation. She wants him to drink from her, fuck her, take her in every way and Grey wants to oblige.

Screams fill the room along with the sound of smashing glass. The blond stripper stands stunned in the doorway for a full thirty seconds before the bouncer arrives.

“Hey, what's going on in--” The bodyguard stops in his tracks watching the horror of Grey feeding from the girl. He launches forward and grabs Grey by the upper arms, “Okay sicko, time to go.”

Grey throws him off with ease, blood dripping from the corner of his mouth. He goes back to finish drinking from her.

Angus approaches Grey cautiously, “Grey, you need to stop. You're going to drain her.”

Grey glances down at Ruby's pale skin, a horrified look of knowing comes over him. “Jesus, what the hell is wrong with me?"

"I don't know, but you'd better get over this fast," Angus says laying Ruby on the couch. "Now fix this and let's get out of--" Angus stops mid-sentence. "Oh for fuck's sake."

Grey looks around, "What?"

"We've got to go." Angus closes the door to the private room and scans the room for another way out.

"I need to take care of this first," Panic rides at the edge of Grey's sanity. He knows he fucked up. Feeding on a human, without permission, in a public place.

"No time," Angus says opening a door at the back of the room. "Let's go."

"No I have to make sure--"

"Now!" Angus demands, "This hallway will get us out of here and away from The Directive agent that just came through the front door."

"Shit!" Grey hisses and follows Angus to the back door.

"Shit is right." Angus shakes his head, "I'd have

been better on my own."

They snake their way down the back hallway and out the door. Grey blanches at the smell when they spill out at the back of the building.

"What the hell is that stench?" Angus puts his hand over his nose and mouth.

"Death." Grey answers, he follows his nose to the dumpster. He peers over the top to see the bodies of two men. Both with puncture wounds on their necks. He turns to Angus in a panic, "What do we do?"

"We get the fuck out of here." Angus runs toward the front of the building and comes to a halt. "Shite!"

Grey's right behind him, bumping into him "You dolt."

Angus shushes him, "We're on foot." And takes off in the other direction.

Grey looks to see three men in the parking lot, one of them standing by his car. He turns heading away from the scene. He passes Angus with ease and stops several blocks away. "Why are we running?"

"Because they're local Directive operatives," Angus says out of breath.

"I've done nothing wrong." Grey insists.

"You fed from a human that's not 'in the program', and there are two bodies in the dumpster with vamp marks in their neck. That's what you've done wrong." Angus paces the sidewalk.

Grey huffs a laugh, "I'm letting myself get caught up in your panic."

"My panic is real. Those Directive guys don't screw around, and now it's going to look like you did the two stiffs in the dumpster." Angus waves his hands wildly.

"I didn't." Grey says with certainty, "And surely I can handle the slap on the wrist for the girl."

"I don't think you know how things work down here," Angus says disgusted. "They like to keep things on the down low. No visits from the home office, if you know what I mean."

"I can understand that, but honestly, I don't

believe this will warrant a trip from home office." Grey smiles at Angus' panic.

"Charles didn't really fill you in did he?" Angus laughs at Grey's ignorance.

"Just that Michael was wreaking havoc." Grey shrugs. "Simple, we apprehend him, turn him in or get him to the Company safehouse. Tell the locals, problem solved."

"You're a sucker." Angus laughs. "Charles didn't tell you that Michael's been good for at least four bodies a night, this shits making the news right now. Exsanguinations on the rise in Atlanta are not the kind of headlines The Directive is willing to tolerate. I heard that Clarence Collins himself may be coming here." Angus' eyes widen, "Clarence fucking Collins."

"He's just a vampire." Grey scoffs.

"Only one of the most powerful vampires in the world." Angus shakes his head, "You may not be phased by this, but I am, and you should be. I know you've been around for a long time, but I doubt you're any match for Clarence."

"I'm not concerned about matching anyone, least of all Clarence Collins. I'm here to control a young vampire for a friend. I'll be happy to explain that to Clarence, I've had many conversations with him, and he's quite the gentleman." Grey says with relief in his tone.

"I can see it now, 'Yeah the stripper that was me, but the stiffs in the dumpster that was Charles' latest convert'."

"If I do have to explain it, that's a perfectly good explanation," Grey says walking back toward the club. "This is foolish, I have nothing to hide. You're welcome to join me, or you can stay here, it's of no consequence to me which you choose."

"You aren't concerned about what's going to happen to you if you don't take care of this for Charles?" Angus follows Grey down the sidewalk.

"Not one bit. I'm tired of being Charles' clean-up crew. Perhaps some time spent with The Directive would be best for him." Grey says unceremoniously.

Angus is horrified by Grey's words, "Grey, what's

gotten into you? You're feeding from humans, having sex with them and now you don't care what happens to your father?"

Grey spins around grabbing Angus by the collar, "Don't you forget that first and foremost, I'm a vampire."

Angus's chest tightens, and he replies without blinking, "I'll never forget it now."

Grey drops him and continues back toward his car. He feels like he could crawl out of his skin, he's parched, angry and needs to fuck. Now.

Chapter Four

Mila sits at the poker table sipping her wine with a belly full of blood and pocket full of cash. *Humans are so easy,* she thinks to herself as she tosses a chip across the table pushing her raven black hair over her shoulder. She considers how to spend the evening, she already knows she'll need to move on from this club and go to the next.

She writhes in her chair as a warm sensation rolls through her body. She lets out a hum as her core swells. All work and no play makes Mila a dull girl. She thinks about the prospect of finding companionship for the evening.

Mila stiffens at smelling a vampire nearby. “Shit.” She hisses feeling him draw closer. She closes her eyes and phases out, transporting herself outside the door in time to watch a frantic vampire swing the door open to the room she was in. He stalks in like a rabid animal.

Time for my exit, she heads quietly for the door wondering if they were Directive. She's been pretty discreet, no one knows what she is and she's been pretty good at keeping it that way. But perhaps not careful enough.

Her steps become sluggish the further away from the room she gets. There’s something drawing her back in that direction, but fear of being caught propel her forward. She gets outside feeling the need for more blood. The thought of it trickling down her throat sends heat spiraling between her thighs.

The night is young, she thinks, looking across the street with thirst parching her throat. She's driven to feed, driven to feel, driven to fuck, but can't seem to make her feet move any further away from the front door of the club.

She wants to go back in, see that vamp again, who was he? What was he doing here if he wasn't Directive?

She paces outside the club for a moment when the scent of a werewolf catches her attention. They'll know what she is the moment they smell her, and she can't take that chance. She disappears quickly to hide out for the evening. It will be safer that way.

"You're back," Hera says in a biting tone as Mila enters the hotel suite.

"Yeah," she throws her purse on the wet bar, "And what have you done all day while I was out working."

"You're looking at it," Hera says popping a chocolate into her mouth.

"You're welcome, by the way." She rolls her eyes

and heads for the bedroom.

"For what?" Hera goes to stand, but decides better of it, she'd let herself go a bit over the years feeding on more than just blood, she has a sweet tooth and isn't afraid to sate it. "You going out, having fun, feeding all day."

Mila stops in the doorway of the bedroom, "I'll have you know if it weren't for my being out 'having fun' as you put it, your ass would be sitting back in the Underworld."

"Both of our asses would be in the Underworld. You should be thanking me, you never would've been able to cross over without me. Cerberus would've seen to that." She turns back toward the TV, "Quit your bitching, I gave you the bigger bedroom."

Mila feels an incredible anger taking over, she's fighting against the urge to jump on Hera and beat her. She shakes her head, what the hell is wrong with me?

Mila looks at the bed calling to her but decides to wash the smell of the strip club off before climbing between the sheets.

In the shower she lets the water course over her skin, thoughts of the vampire from the club invade her thoughts. He was delicious. His movements smooth and deliberate. Those intense eyes. She's feeling lost in them, even though she only saw them for a split second as he flashed by her.

She moves her hands over her body, to her thighs and between her folds to her most sensitive parts. She can feel herself swollen, wet and needy for him, but doesn't understand what's coming over her. Her desire is already constant, and she brushes the feeling off as just being her nature to want him.

Images of him flash through her mind as the heat continues to build in her core. She can feel his hands on her body, getting lost in him.

"Mila, get hold of yourself." She says, pulling herself out of the moment.

Who is he? And what will he do if he finds me?

A Vampire's Thirst

Chapter Five

Grey reaches the parking lot hoping to catch the scent again. There's nothing, the club appears to be closed. Odd at eight thirty at night.

There are two cars left in the parking lot aside from his own. He remembers the bodies in the dumpster and sniffs at the air to see if they're still there. The smell is faint, he's sure they aren't there anymore but goes back to check.

The smell isn't overpowering as he gets closer and sees no reason to check. He turns back for his car, satisfied that the bodies are gone. Probably removed by The Directive.

Another scent, one he's not fond of enters his nostrils. Shit!

"Coming back to the scene of the crime?" A deep gravely voice calls out from behind the dumpster.

"I'm not sure what you mean, wolf," Grey says without fully acknowledging him.

"I think you do." The wolf comes closer to Grey.

"Then you'd be wrong, very wrong." Grey doesn't stop walking away. He'd like to put as much distance between him and the wolf as possible if only to staunch the smell.

"Would I?" The wolf catches up to him.

"Yes," Grey reaches his car and opens the door.

The wolf closes the door before Grey can get in, the bold move shocks Grey. "Excuse me, but I'm leaving."

"After you answer a few questions." The wolf says.

Grey tenses then evaluates his options. He could

kill the wolf, that's certainly an option. Grey narrows his eyes and with a sardonic smile moves toward him.

Angus runs up and stops between Grey and the wolf. "Hey, Vash, how's it going?"

"Angus, I should've known you'd be involved in this," Vash says shaking his head.

"Involved in what?" Angus feigns innocence.

"The two bodies in the dumpster?" Vash scrutinizes Grey, "And the vampire."

"Can't say I know anything about the bodies, but yeah, the vamp is mine," Angus says with a nervous laugh.

Grey cocks his head at Angus, "Yours?"

"Well, what I mean to say is, I'm showing him around. But those guys in the dumpster, not us." Angus holds his hands up in surrender.

"Really? And who is your vampire friend?" Vash quirks his brow.

Grey steps forward, "Grey Hart, you must be relatively new here. I spend quite a lot of time in Atlanta."

"I've been here a little over a year," Vash says with pride.

"Ah, yes, just a blip in time." Grey moves toward his car, "If you'll excuse me."

"I still have some questions for you," Vash says trying to keep Grey from getting in the car.

Grey turns to him with a deep threat in his eyes, "You'd do well to take your hands off the Bentley."

Vash puffs out his chest, "And you'd do well to answer my questions."

"You haven't asked anything." Grey' impatience hangs in the air with an edge to his tone.

"What do you know about the bodies?" Vash asks point blank.

"Not a damn thing," Grey says lowering himself into the car. "Is that it?"

"I'll be in touch," Vash says with warning.

"I'm sure." Grey slams the door closed.

Angus trots around the front of the car and slides into the passenger seat. "I'll see you around, Vash."

Grey calmly pulls the car out of the spot and toward the road. "Who the hell is that asshole?"

"Vash is one of the agents with the Atlanta Directive." Angus says with warning, "You don't want to piss him off."

"Why?" Grey asks with a scary calmness to him.

"Because then we have more of The Directive on our ass, just steer clear, okay?" Angus pleads.

"Fuck him, he better not get in my way," Grey says gripping the steering wheel. "I need to feed."

"Again?" Angus asked annoyed.

"I could always just take your blood." Grey arches his brow.

Angus pulls his collar up closer to his neck, "How about no."

Grey smiles, "Then I'm sure you'll have no objection to me going to the feeding grounds."

"No objection from me, boss," Angus says staring straight ahead through the windshield. "But I do want to get on with finding Michael."

"Dammit!" Grey hits the steering wheel with his fist.

"You forgot didn't you." Angus blows out a frustrated breath "Seriously, what is it with you?"

Grey shakes his head, "I don't know, I just don't feel like myself and this thirst and this." He grips his hard cock in his hand.

"Whoa, I'm not helping you with that either." Angus presses himself against the door, putting distance between them.

"I'm not interested in your help with this." Grey cringes, "But I do think I need to feed before I go out into public again."

"Maybe that will help." Angus taps his finger to his chin, "Let's go back to the hotel, you can feed, we can regroup."

"Good idea." Grey nods. He really can't quite figure out what's wrong. He hasn't had trouble with any of those types of urges in a very long time. Before this morning, he hadn't fed from a live human for nearly a hundred years.

The watch in his pocket tickles at the back of his mind. It's always what he goes back to when he considers feeding on a live human.

Chapter Six

"Where are you going now?" Hera asks sitting in the same position on the couch.

"Back out, we need at least five thousand, so I'm going to make some money tonight." Mila throws her purse over her shoulder.

"You're going to end up getting us caught," Hera says mostly disinterested.

"What's it to you, anyway?" Mila says in a hurt tone, "You're just sitting here doing nothing."

"You're the one that's on the run." Hera snaps back. "I'd be sitting at home all comfy cozy if you weren't trying to get away from Elomere."

"Elomere isn't the only reason we came up." Mila flips her long black hair over her shoulder.

"If you want to go back, I can be ready...now." Hera stands up from the couch.

Mila hangs her head, she doesn't want to go back to the Underworld. Hera knows it and is banking on it.

"That's what I thought." Hera sits back down. "You know, there are worse fates than having to be paired with Elomere."

"No, not many. He's arrogant, inconsiderate and I just plain don't like him. All the women can fawn over him, and they can also have him. He's cruel to me, Hera and the thought of spending eternity with him as his primary mate makes me wish I could die." Mila opens the door to their hotel suite. "I really don't see what everyone sees in him. He's just another pretty face and a puppet."

"A puppet that can give you a life of luxury." Hera points out.

"Not everyone wants that. I want happiness, love,

passion and so much more than just a luxurious life. I don't want to live as one of many lovers, I want to be with one man and be his only woman" Her voice is pleading.

"That is ridiculous, besides, would you really be willing to give up your hunky feeding partner? Ty is quite the gift to women." Hera pumps her brow.

Mila shakes her head, "I'll be back later, but you should make sure you're ready to go when we get back. We're going to need to move on soon."

"Great, I'll be ready," Hera says not looking away from the TV. "And if you want to go back, I'll open the portal anytime."

Mila walks down the hallway of the hotel to the stairwell. "I wish I didn't need her. Why can't I open the portal?" She's one of the only blood fairies that haven't been able to master the art of portals. Probably her father's doing so he can keep her in the Underworld.

Mila stands outside the strip club and adjusts her white thigh high stockings under her long trench coat. She walks through the door and finds the bouncer, "Hey there. Can I talk to the manager?"

"Looking for a job?" The tall, beefy man says.

"Yeah, just temporary." She says ticking her head.

"Dancer or waitress?" He walks away and indicates for her to follow.

"Dancer." Mila looks around the dimly lit club. There are men sitting at the tables with eyes focused on the beautiful blonds on the stage. She can hear their blood pumping through their veins, and she's reminded that she needs to feed. But not yet, she has to wait.

"Hey, Georgie." The bouncer calls to the man behind the bar with a belly that always arrives before he does.

"Yeah?" Georgie answers impatiently.

"Got a dancer." The bouncer motions to Mila and heads back for the door.

Mila smiles and reaches to shake his hand. He doesn't take it. "You danced before?"

Mila nods, "Yeah."

Georgie ticks his head, "What have you got, open the coat."

His eyes widen when she opens her coat. He slowly scans her from head to toe. "Very nice."

"Thank you." Mila smiles with a rush of power knowing that he'll give her anything she wants. At the core, she enjoys this game. Getting men to give her money.

"Okay, go in the back and talk to Candy, she'll put you in the lineup for tonight. If you do okay, we'll keep you." He waves her to the back and tries to turn away.

Her eyes soften to a sultry gaze, "Thank you, Georgie."

"You're welcome." He sputters. "Yeah, you can..."

She puts her finger over his lips, "I know I can." She turns on her heel and heads for the back. That's the rush she loves, getting them hot and walking away. It's an addiction for her. She needs it almost as much as she needs blood.

She gets to the back and scans the room for a girl

that looks like she's in charge. There's a woman that was once probably quite pretty, but time has not been kind to her. "Are you Candy?"

"Yeah, who's asking?" She says while picking up clothes off one of the couches in the back lounge area.

"I'm Mila, Georgie said to talk to you about being in the lineup tonight." Mila looks around at the lit vanities for one that's not cluttered with makeup.

"Well, Georgie can suck it. There's no room in the lineup." Candy doesn't look up at Mila.

Mila knows this will require a little more persuasion than Georgie, "Surely you can squeeze me in."

Candy stops and lifts her eyes to Mila, she takes her in as Mila slides her coat off her shoulders. Mila slowly walks closer to Candy and slides her finger down Candy's bare arm. "I'm sure you have room."

Candy sucks in a breath, "I don't.." She trails off.

Mila licks her lips getting closer to Candy's ear, her finger trails down in front and she gently presses against her clit through her panties. "Don't what?" Mila challenges working her clit harder.

Candy's breathing becomes erratic. Mila licks Candy's earlobe, "You can squeeze me in."

"Yeah, I'll squeeze you in." Candy agrees.

Mila steps away from her, leaving Candy cold. "Thank you. What's the split?"

Candy takes a moment to recover, catching her breath, "The Club gets ten percent, I get five, got it?"

"Yes, ma'am," Mila says with a bounce.

"What's your name?" Candy asks.

"I told you, I'm Mila."

"Is that your real name or what you dance under?" Candy says studying her with lustful eyes.

"My real name." Mila nods.

"Your new name is Siren." Candy brushes past her nearly recovered from the hot encounter. "Any particular songs you dance to?"

"Nope, I can dance to anything with a beat." Mila smiles.

"Okay, I'll get you in on the next set, until then make yourself at home and get ready." Candy stops taking in Mila's shape, "You're going to make some money tonight!"

"I hope so," Mila says with a twinkle in her eye.

"How long have you been dancing?" Candy asks.

"Not long. But I like it. I like feeling sexy." Mila shrugs.

"You are sexy," Candy's eyes rake Mila's body. "If you'd like to get together after closing..."

"I'd like that." Mila nods, knowing she'll be long gone at closing.

"You like making money." Candy raises her brow.

"That too." Mila agrees.

"I'm surprised some sugar daddy hasn't come along and snatched you up."

"I'm not one to be owned." Mila lowers her head, "Back home...let's just say my betrothed is a man of great means."

"But he just doesn't stoke your fire, huh?" Candy laments the thought leaving Mila wondering if Candy can relate.

"No, he's arrogant and possessive. I can't see myself with someone like that." Mila says with a stream of worry that Elomere could be getting closer to finding her.

"Remember, hun, no matter where you go, there you are. You can't run forever." Candy says waving a finger.

"Who says I'm running?" Mila's taken aback by Candy's frankness.

"That scared look in your eye and the need to rake in cash fast." Candy takes a few steps toward Mila, "Did he beat you?"

Mila ticks her head back, "No. My father would've had him beheaded."

"Protective Daddy, huh?" Candy huffs a laugh.

Mila giggles internally realizing that Candy thinks she's exaggerating. "Something like that. It's not okay to hit women in my culture."

"It's not okay in my culture either, but it still happens all the time." Candy says rolling her eyes.

"You've been beaten by a man?" Mila's shocked, "And he lived?"

"Yes, and they're all still alive and well." Candy steps away and turns for the door.

"Did you ever fight back?" Mila asks feeling completely incensed that anyone would lay a hand on Candy. She seems so kind but understands why she's jaded.

"If by fighting back, you mean running away, then yes." Candy turns and looks back at Mila, "Get ready for your set and knock em dead."

Mila considers Candy's story, she wants to know more about it. She wants to defend her, avenge her in some way. She's knows this is a very different world than her own, but she can't imagine a place where someone would get away with beating another person. Where she's from, they handle things in a civilized manner, a fight to the death.

This is one crazy world these humans have, she thinks to herself.

Chapter Seven

Grey busts through the door to his hotel suite with a cold sweat forming on his brow. He goes to the couch and looks back at Angus. "I need to feed."

"I got you," Angus brings a bag to Grey. "Here you go."

Grey gulps directly from the bag finishing it and feels immediately unsatisfied. "Ugh, this is awful. It's cold."

"Well, yeah it's cold. Do we need to go to a feeding ground?" Angus asks full of concern.

Grey shakes his head, "No, I don't know what's wrong with me. I've been fine on donor blood for a very long time. But right now, I need warm blood flowing down my throat..."

"Hey, stay with me," Angus says snapping his fingers. "We need to figure out what's wrong with you. Today you were feeding on a live donor directly."

"It's been nearly a hundred years." Grey rakes his fingers through his hair. "I don't understand."

"It's only going to get worse with nightfall." Angus sits on the couch next to him.

"I'm not sure how it can get worse," Grey's eyes widen and tries to shift his hard cock in his pants, "Blood isn't the only thing I'm craving. I feel like I'm going to go insane if I don't have what I want."

"You've got to get hold of yourself. Could this be some sort of infection? A bad batch of blood? Did Charles do something to you?" Angus tries to come up with an explanation.

"I don't know." Grey looks at Angus with desperation in his eyes, "You've got to help me."

"I don't know how to help you. I can bring you all the live donors that are willing to help you with both of your needs, but save you from it...that's not my specialty." Angus ticks his head towards Grey's pants.

"What the fuck good are you?" Grey stands from the couch and goes to the balcony for fresh air. It does nothing to soothe him. So many heartbeats in the city, and he can hear them all.

The madness is taking him over.

He closes his eyes and tries to regain control. The sweet scent catches his attention, familiar and intoxicating. He has to find the source. He goes back into the room. "We've got to go."

"What?" Angus says in a panic, "You're in no condition to go anywhere. Your face is all..." He makes a circle around his own face and cringes. "Vampire-ey."

Grey takes another bag of blood and drinks it down. It does nothing to soothe his burning need, either of them. He's rubs himself and knows he needs to have some sort of release soon or there are going to be consequences.

He looks at Angus, then the door.

"I know what you're thinking right now, Grey and you're right. I'm no match for you. I'm not as strong, fast or deadly. So I'm asking you as your friend, don't put me in that position." Angus pleads with seriousness in his tone. "I'm just trying to keep you from doing something I know you're going to regret."

Angus' tone reaches a small part of Grey before he gets to the door. He doesn't say a word, ready to snap and trying his level best not to. He reaches into his pocket and pulls out the pocket watch. Grey runs his finger over the inscription on the inside cover. *"Time has a way of showing us what really matters."*

He exhales, able to center himself for a brief moment. His phone dings in his pocket, a notification of an email.

"Melanie," Grey hesitates on opening up the email.

"Who's Melanie?" Angus asks intrigued.

"One of my students. She's apparently done with her paper. She always sends them to me before submitting them through the system." Grey's irritation is apparent.

"I don't really care what all that means," Angus says realizing that the email brought Grey back to himself. "Why don't you read it?"

"I guess I can look it over," Grey says ready to open the document.

"It seems to be calming you down." Angus remarks.

"Yeah, it's a good reminder of why I try to always do the right thing." Grey nods affirmation as the document opens on his phone.

> *Professor Hart,*
>
> *I hope you enjoy my paper. If you have any suggestions before I submit it, please let me know.*
>
> *Melanie.*

"Aw, isn't that sweet, she uses a little heart for

the A in your name." Angus teases.

"Melanie's definitely special." Grey rolls his eyes and takes a glimpse at the paper.

Passion and desire, a thirst that can only be quenched by your one true love...

"Oh my God that's it." Grey stands from the couch and begins to pace.

"What's it?" Angus is lost.

"The Thirst. I have the Thirst." Grey says waving his hands.

"Well, we knew that." Angus twists his expression with sarcasm.

"It's very rare." Grey breathes the words out, "It can't be, though."

"The Thirst? Nah, I've seen lots of vamps crazy with hunger." Angus waves Grey's words off.

"No, no." Grey inhales an impatient breath, "When a vampire is near their Bloodmate, they get the Thirst. It can only be sated by finding their Bloodmate."

"So you mean to tell me that there's some Vamp-tart running around that we have to find?" Angus asks. "Crazed with this Thirst?"

"Don't talk about my Bloodmate that way." Grey balls his fists at his sides.

"Sorry, just trying to figure all of this out." Angus holds his hands up in surrender.

"We have to find her." Grey starts for the door.

"Whoa, whoa, what about Michael?" Angus stands in front of the door.

"Fuck Michael," A flare of anger runs through Grey.

"Hold on. We have to --"

"No, we have to find her. I have to find my Bloodmate." Grey goes to the door with purpose.

"Any ideas where to start?" Angus asks following behind him.

"None. But I know her scent. That's where I need to start." He opens the door and is startled seeing Vash standing on the other side. He's rarely surprised, especially by a werewolf. *I've got to get on my game,* he thinks to himself.

"On your way to wreak more havoc?" Vash asks looking Grey dead in the eye.

"I'm not sure what you mean, but you should get the fuck out of my way," Grey tries to push past him, and Vash puts his hand on Grey's chest.

"I'm onto you. I've got seven bodies, all drained, all vamp attacks and everything leads back to you." The threat in Vash's tone insites Grey.

Grey grabs Vash's hand and bends it all the way back putting him on his knees. "Listen to me, dog. I haven't killed anyone..." He lowers himself closer to Vash's ear. "Yet."

Vash remains silent, apparently smart enough to know when he's out of his league.

"That's what I thought." Grey releases him and goes to the elevator. "Fuck this."

Grey leaves in a flash down the stairs, much faster than the elevator.

When he reaches the lobby, he doesn't slow down leaving nothing but a breeze in his wake.

He gets to the streets, deciding to forego the car so that he can try to pick up on her scent. Her delightful bouquet. He stands for a moment, hoping the inspiration will come to him on which direction to go.

Angus comes out the revolving door of the hotel room, "Grey."

"What!" Grey answers irritated.

"I think we need to either decide to abandon Michael or go find him. I know you need to find this mate of yours, but the body count is rising. The Directive is going to send someone bigger than locals if it doesn't stop." Angus pleads.

"That does not concern me," Grey says trying to focus on her scent.

"It should," Angus says with a seriousness he's not heard from him before.

Grey looks down at Angus, "Why?"

"If this Thirst thing affects your Bloodmate the same way it's affecting you..." Angus asks hoping Grey will understand.

Grey lifts his head in thought, "Oh, I..I believe it could. If she's a vampire."

"Right, what if it's not Michael doing all of the

killing? What if your Bloodmate doesn't have hundreds of years of control under her belt?" Angus brings up the point.

"If it is her doing the killing we've got to get to her. Once we're together, the Thirst will subside." Grey says with more determination in his voice than before.

"So, we need Vash to find out where the bodies have been found and what leads he has, to beat him to her," Angus explains.

It all makes sense, but one thing, "But Vash thinks I'm doing it?"

"Vash believes you *could* be doing it, there's a difference. He still has information we need, and we need to keep home office Directive out of here. It could be dangerous for you, her and Michael." Angus says looking back toward the door where Vash is coming out.

Grey nods his approval.

"Hey Vash," Angus approaches him with his hands clasped together, "I've talked with Grey, he's just been a little on edge, so let's see what we can do to help. We don't want some rogue vamp out on the streets. Grey understands it gives them all a bad name."

"So he's ready to give me some information?" Vash asks looking at Grey with disdain.

"Yes, of course. I'm eager to assist you in your investigation. Specifically, since I have nothing to hide." Grey approaches Vash. He's trying not to visibly let his skin crawl at the thought of being this close to a wolf.

"How long have you been in Atlanta?" Vash asks.

"Not even one full day," Grey answers politely. "How long have the killings been going on?"

"For about four days." Vash answers. "How many humans have you fed on since you got here."

"Two. Willing donors." Grey answers wishing he could calm the erection in his pants at the thought of fulfilling that need too. "Where are you finding the bodies?"

"All in dumpsters behind strip clubs. With the

exception of one. One we found behind a hotel." Vash contemplates the different location of the body. "It could be unrelated."

"But you're sure it's a vampire?" Grey asks.

"Positive," Vash says.

"At which hotel did you find the body?" Grey asks, the gears turning in his head. It would be quite convenient if he could find his Bloodmate there.

"The Hyatt on Peachtree." Vash answers.

"That's not far from here." Grey taps his finger on his chin.

"Okay, so Grey, you want to get started?" Angus asks tugging at Grey's jacket.

"I think we should --" Vash starts.

"Split up," Grey says as though it's final.

"I think we should stay together. It'll be better for information sharing." Vash takes a step toward Grey.

"I believe that if a vampire is involved, I'll be far more likely to get cooperative answers than a wolf." Grey says walking past Vash, "Angus and I will work independently from you, but we will share information. We'll check in no later than sun up."

"Where are you heading? I don't want to duplicate our efforts." Vash calls after Grey.

"To the Hyatt." Grey says without turning around, "You should look into the victim's, find out if they have anything in common."

"I'll hear from you before sunrise?" Vash yells down the street.

"Yes." Grey waves his hand over his shoulder. He continues down the street with purpose. He has to resist the urge to use his vampire speed and drain one of the passers-by.

"You okay there?" Angus asks studying Grey's face.

"I'm alright." Grey grinds out, trying to control all of his urges.

"Because I've never seen a vampire sweat before and I'm a little nervous you won't be able to hold it together," Angus says cautiously.

"I'm fine." Grey's jaw pops with tension."This

slow pace is killing me, I could be there already."

"Just keep your pace, we don't want to upset the delicate balance," Angus warns.

Grey sniffs at the air, the faint scent of her urges him on faster. Angus is having to work to keep up. "She's close."

"We're almost at the Hyatt." Angus has a pang of hesitance in his tone.

They walk into the lobby straight to the stairs. "You seem to know where you're going," Angus asks with an air of questioning.

"I'm following her trail." At the fifth floor, Grey busts through the door to the corridor. He walks with purpose toward her scent. When he gets to room Fifty-three thirty-seven he inhales deeply, her scent filling all of him. Heat spirals through him straight to his shaft at the thought of her being so close. He reaches down for the doorknob.

"Hey!" Angus stops him, "You should really knock."

"Why? My Bloodmate is here. She will want me to come in, find her and take her." Grey's eyes are glossing over at the prospect of having her in his arms and drinking her sweet blood.

"What if you're wrong?" Angus asks considering the disaster if he's wrong.

"I'm not." He says with certainty. He pauses for a moment realizing the scent is dwindling. He lifts his hand from the knob and knocks on the door.

"I'll play it safe." He looks down at Angus as he waits impatiently for the door to open.

"Thank you," Angus says looking nervously down the hall.

"No one's answering." Grey glances at Angus as though he'll know what to do.

"Knock again," Angus states the obvious.

"Screw this." Grey reaches down and turns the knob hard enough for the locks to disengage. He pushes through the door to see something he wasn't expecting.

On the couch of the hotel suite is an older woman with greying hair, very plain watching TV and eating pizza.

"Who the hell are you?" She stands up holding

her palms toward him defensively.

"I'm Grey." Confusion rattles his being, he feels nothing for this woman standing in front of him. He can still smell the mixture of his Bloodmate's scent, but it's been completely adulterated by this woman.

"What the fuck are you doing breaking in here?" The woman takes two steps back still holding her hands in front of her.

"I was looking for someone," Grey says in a half daze.

"Elomere sent you didn't he?" She hisses, "Well, you're out of luck, she isn't here."

"I don't know who Elomere is." Grey's confusion coupled with his increasing inability to maintain focus is wearing on him.

"Sure you don't." She puts her hand on her hip.

Angus comes in the room, "She's not here, mate, let's go."

"Yeah, get out of here." The woman sneers.

Angus sees the woman and a smile lights his features, "Hey there."

"Seriously? A brownie? I can do way better than that." She rolls her eyes.

"I'll have you know --" Angus starts defensively.

"Enough, I need to find her. Who is she?" Grey takes a few steps toward the woman.

Panic fills her expression, and she vanishes.

"What the hell?" Grey moves to the spot she was standing in.

"Where'd she go?" Angus says looking around the room.

Grey searches the other rooms in the suite. He can smell that she was here, but she's gone now. He reaches the main room of the suite where Angus is still trying to find the woman. "She's not here."

"What the hell was that woman? I mean, can vamps just disappear?" Angus says peeking out onto the balcony.

"Not that I'm aware of, but there are many different abilities among us. But she wasn't a vampire." Grey taps his finger to his chin.

"How do you know? She didn't give you the secret handshake?" Angus chuckles at his own joke.

"No, she was eating pizza. Vampires don't eat." Grey says feeling his control waning even more. "I have to find her, Angus."

"Okay, any ideas?" Angus says with concern.

"I can try to pick up her scent, but I think we should head to the strip clubs." Grey passes by Angus on the way out the door. "I'll meet you there."

"Don't you think we should stay together?" Angus jogs to keep up.

"You're too slow, and I can't wait much longer," Grey says with urgency.

"We can drive." Angus says looking down, "And honestly, I think you need supervision."

"I don't need a Goddamn thing from you." Grey bellows and immediately apologizes. "I'm sorry, I'm just..."

"On edge. I get it. But this is why we need to stick together. I can run interference, be a voice of reason." Angus continues to follow Grey down the stairwell.

"Just try to keep up." Grey's more determined

than ever to find her. He knows his sanity is slipping away and the only cure is finding her.

A Vampire's Thirst

Chapter Eight

Mila sits at the vanity getting ready for her chance to dance and make some money and maybe even feed. She understands economy, but where she comes from everything is paid for in favors of some sort. That's the currency. But with enough money, she'll be able to solve her Elomere problem for good.

Who the hell does he think he is anyway, as though she would bind herself to anyone, especially him. He's arrogant, piggish and not nearly as good looking as he thinks he is. No, she's not looking for a man like that, regardless of tradition, her father or anyone back home. She's going to make sure she can stay here if only to escape having to be Elomere's primary, or worse, his second. "I'm nobody's second." She sneers.

She squirms a little in her chair feeling a hot rush come over her. It's been happening a lot today, and she's insatiably hungry for blood.

"Okay, cupcake, you're up." One of the other dancers taps her on the shoulder as she walks by. "Watch out for the big guy in the front, he's a little handsy."

"I'm Siren." She says confused by the woman calling her cupcake.

"Yeah, you're adorable. Get out there and shake your ass." She says sliding a robe over her shoulders.

"Thanks." Mila checks her appearance in the mirror one more time before heading for the stage.

The music pumps through the speakers, and her body moves with the beat. She's feeling hella sexy tonight and might just decide to do more than just feed on blood.

Men line the stage with money in their hands, she evaluates which ones have dollar bills or twenties. She'll only dance for the high money. She works the pole on the stage wetting their appetites as well as her own.

Heat is running through her with a burning desire, she needs a hard cock and warm blood to fill all of her.

Mila's lust is colliding in a dangerous culmination of lack of judgement. She brings her focus back, *Mila, you need to make money. Do that, make money.*

She moves down toward the men to start collecting her money. The big guy in the front is holding twenties. She dances, just for him as he slides twenty after twenty into her g-string.

He can't take his eyes off her, she's driving him wild, she can see the erection bulging from his pants, she wants it. In a matter of moments, he'll be hers to do whatever she pleases.

The music comes to a stop, and the DJ comes over

the loudspeaker, "Let's give it up for Siren."

The crowd cheers and Mila gives the big man in the front one last wink.

He crooks his finger for her to come closer and whispers in her ear, "You want to make this a private party?"

Mila looks toward the private rooms, "I'd love to."

"I'll meet you in VIP room two." He pumps his brow with excitement.

Mila goes to the back and sits at the vanity. She knows better than to count her money right there in front of everyone. But she's certain she made a good haul, and she's about to hit the motherload.

"You really impressed big Doug." One of the girls says, "Did he invite you to a 'private party'?"

"Yeah, I'm just going to get my stuff put up and head over to the room." Mila puts her money in her bag, puts it in the locker Candy assigned to her and places a protection trap on the lock.

"Watch him, he likes to touch and break the rules." The girl says filing her nails.

"I can handle him," Mila says with confidence.

Candy comes in the back, "Be careful, remember, nothing illegal and no touching."

"Got it, I have no intentions on letting him touch me." Mila ticks her chin downward. "I'm not about all that."

"Good girl." Candy says with confidence.

Mila struts toward the private room. The bouncer standing outside the room stops her, "If you need any help or things get out of hand, I'm right here. Just let out a holler."

"Got it, but I'm sure it'll be okay." Mila smiles and walks through the door.

"Hello," Mila says in a sultry tone approaching him.

"Hello, beautiful. I'm Doug." He eyes her from head to toe.

"It's a pleasure to meet you," Mila holds out her hand.

Doug hesitates, "There's no touching."

Mila lowers her eyes to him, "It's just a handshake." She needs to make contact with him to be sure her spell takes, he can't remember anything about her. He will feel no pain and just be short the money in his pocket and some blood in his veins.

"If you're okay with it." He takes her hand. His eyes gloss over slightly, "You are so soft."

Mila smiles. "Thank you. So would you like to start with a lap dance?" She begins to slide off her sparkly bra.

Doug's eyes widen, "You're so beautiful."

"Thank you." Mila clicks play on the iPod sitting in a cradle on one of the tables. Sexy music fills the small room, and she begins to dance.

She's not attracted to Doug at all, but she can feel heat pooling between her legs. A burning desire to feel the length of him inside her and release a powerful orgasm is taking over. She shakes the thought away to keep on the task at hand. She needs to feed and get paid. That's all that matters, she starts chanting to herself.

She can feel him wanting to touch her, he's hypnotized. He's right where she needs him. She goes in closer to him, holding his gaze. He lurches toward her, his lips ready to crash over hers.

She darts slightly to the side and kisses his neck gently before sinking her teeth into him.

A Vampire's Thirst

Chapter Nine

Grey steps out of the car and sniffs at the air. “She’s close, she’s here.” he stalks toward the door with Angus in tow.

“Calm down, you need to play it cool. We’re here to find Michael too, don’t forget.” Angus says struggling to keep up with Grey’s pace.

“Who?” Grey says not slowing down.

“Michael, the whole reason you're here.” Angus rolls his eyes. “I really do hope she’s in there so you can get back to your right mind.”

“She is, I can feel her.” Grey tries to ignore the

throbbing between his legs. He has to have her, now. He needs to feel her sweet blood trickling down his throat while he pushes himself into her inviting cleft.

"Grey!" Angus raises his voice. "Stay with me."

"I am trying." Grey grinds out.

They reach the door, and the bouncer asks for their ID's, "That'll be Twenty bucks each."

Grey slides a hundred dollar bill out of his wallet and throws it at the man pushing past him. The guy looks at the bill, then Grey and shrugs, pocketing the change.

She's so close, Grey doesn't stop to look for her, he's drawn to her. He stalks toward the back of the club to the VIP rooms going through the main door into a hallway filled with rooms covered by red curtains.

He finds the one with the bouncer outside. "Fuck off." He waves his hand in front of the bouncer's face.

Absently the muscle-bound man walks away down the hall.

Grey throws the red curtain aside to see a small woman struggling under a huge middle-aged man.

Grey's immediately incensed, rage coursing through him. He pulls the man off with ease. Still holding the perpetrator by the back of his collar, he sees her, smells her, needs her. “Are you okay?” He drops the man on the floor like an old bag of trash.

She looks at him wide-eyed and frightened trying to wipe the blood from her lips. “I-I-” She sputters.

Grey moves his hand toward the blood on her lips “You're hurt.”

Her entire body begins to quiver, and she disappears before Grey's eyes. He moves to where she was on the couch and looks around frantically. “Fuck!”

“Um, Grey,” Angus says with warning.

“Did you see where she went?” Grey asks in a panic. “I have to find her.”

“We've got another problem.” Angus motions down at the man with two puncture wounds in his neck, “I don't think she was the victim.”

Grey inhales a deep contemplative breath, “A

vampire, she's definitely a vampire."

"Are you sure? She disappeared like the one in the hotel." Angus remarks with a tick of his head.

"It doesn't matter, I have to find her." He turns to leave.

"Hey, what are we going to do about him?" Angus calls after Grey.

Grey blows out an exasperated breath as he notices the club security coming down the hallway. His intense need to protect her drives him back toward the man. He spins around and pushes past Angus, "Get out of the way."

Grey leans down relieved that he can hear a pulse, she didn't take too much. he's going to be fine. He puts too drops of his own blood on the man's puncture wounds to heal them, then wipes away the blood.

Grey lifts him up, "Come on, mate."

The security guard reaches them, "Is everything okay over here?"

"Sure is," Angus says taking the man's other side. "This bloke doesn't know when to stop."

The security guard steps aside and lets Grey and Angus take the man with them.

"What are we going to do with him?" Angus asks huffing under the man's weight.

"Once I'm out the door, I don't care." Grey bites.

Angus stops in his tracks, "What the bloody hell?"

Grey sees a tall, muscular man with long white hair barreling toward him. He grabs Grey by the lapels, "Where is she?"

Grey reacts immediately, dropping Doug and removing the other man's hands from his jacket. He pushes him against the wall and lets his fangs show, "Don't you ever touch me or I'll rip your fucking arms off."

"Grey, come on, calm down." Angus tugs at his sleeve.

The patrons and dancers scatter in the club at the sight, a cacophony of screams and gasps fill the air along with the rush of everyone trying to get out through the small exit.

"Yes, Grey, you should calm down." The man bares his own fangs.

Grey studies him bewildered. He's not a vampire, but what is he. "Who are you?"

"I'm the one who will kill you if you ever lay a hand on Mila." He grinds out pushing Grey back with ease, catching Grey off guard.

He's not accustomed to violence and rarely runs into anyone that can physically move him when he doesn't want to be moved.

"Mila?" Grey whispers, "is that her name?"

"My betrothed. I am Elomere of The Underworld Fae, and she is promised to me." He holds his head high with arrogance.

"I don't give two shits who you are." Grey attacks him with speed and acuity. He's stronger and faster than Elomere slamming him into the wall. Drywall and dust crumble behind him.

Elomere recovers quickly and goes straight for Grey's throat. Grey dodges him swinging him around by the arm into the wall across the club. Tables and chairs go airborne as rage courses through Grey, like he's never felt before. He's lost all control, and he will see Elomere dead.

He slowly stalks across the room looking Elomere in the eyes, "You've made a grave mistake."

"Grey!" Angus calls out from across the club. He's trying to get to the bouncer before the bouncer gets to Grey.

Grey turns around and grabs the bouncer by the head ready to twist and break his neck.

Angus comes to a halt next to Grey, "Grey, stop!"

Grey pauses, his chest heaving with the desire to destroy anything in his way from finding his Bloodmate.

"If you do this, it's all over," Angus warns him, trying to talk him off the ledge.

Grey's breathing doesn't regulate, he continues to imagine the bouncers head all but disconnected from his body so he can drink freely on his blood.

"But, I have to --"

"Have to what?" Vash's voice fills the room with warning. "Kill him? Drink from him? I don't think that would be wise."

Grey releases the bouncer, "Go outside."

The bouncer makes for the door in a half daze.

"I'd like to know what you were doing?" Vash approaches Grey. "I thought you weren't going to be a problem."

"I'm not the problem, it's..." Grey turns toward Elomere to find he's gone.

"It's what?" Vash asks expectantly.

"Blood fairy." Angus chimes in. "There was a blood fairy here, Grey was trying to stop him from feeding on this guy. I'm thinking he's the one responsible for your killings."

Grey marvels at how fast Angus is on his feet with the lies and diversions.

"Blood fae? How do you know?" Vash looks around the empty club.

"He said he was from The Underworld," Grey says a matter of factly. "We were following a lead here. Found the guy drinking this guy nearly dry." Grey motions to Doug still unconscious on the floor.

"Where is the blood fairy now?" Vash asks.

"He disappeared, they can do that," Angus says with authority.

"But why would a Blood fairy be here, they are

strictly forbidden." Vash blows out a breath. "This is much worse than I thought. I'm going to have to bring in the home office, now we're talking treaty violations."

"Vash," Angus reaches up to put his arm across Vash's shoulders, "Don't be so hasty."

"I have to report this," Vash says with certainty.

"You can report it, but first why don't you catch him. *You* stop the killing, *you* catch the bad guy, and the home office will know *you've* got your city under control." Angus plays on Vash's ego.

Vash takes a moment to think about it, "I have to call it in now."

"Suit yourself. But, do you really want Clarence Collins all up in your business?" Angus sidles up to Vash, "Now that I think about it...you really don't want Clarence sniffing around here."

Vash considers Angus' warning. "I think we can hold off. But we have to wrap this up fast."

Grey struggles to maintain his control. All of his needs and desires are taking over, driving him and he won't stop until he gets what he wants. He walks away from Angus and Vash toward his car without saying a word. He has to get away from this place and toward her. Wherever she is.

Grey starts the car, and Angus knocks on the window, "Let me in."

Grey unlocks the door, and Angus slides in, "What was that?"

"I have to find her." He says with determination.

"Yeah, you're not going to find her if you end up in The Directive's crosshairs." Angus' irritation comes through in his tone.

"Fuck The Directive." Grey grinds out.

"Fuck you. You've got me all bound up in this." Angus shakes his head, "Let's just find Michael, then we can find your mystery girl."

"First, Charles got you bound up in this. Not me." Grey pulls out onto the road, "Second..." He pauses and releases a breath, "I can't control this thing burning inside me. I have to find her, or it's not going to be good for anyone."

"Just settle down," Angus says holding his hands up. "If we look at this logically, we can assume we could find her at another strip club."

"What makes you say that?" Grey asks, offended that his Bloodmate would be so deeply involved in strip clubs.

"Because she's in it for the blood and the money," Angus says.

"You don't know that." Grey grips the steering wheel to bear the brunt of his anger.

"I do, and honestly, it's brilliant. She finds a mark with some money, feeds from a willing donor and then lifts their cash." Angus is impressed with the scam, "The simplicity is beautiful."

"You think she's stealing from them?" Grey asks astonished.

"Yeah, first she's a blood fairy, the guys have no idea they're being fed from. That's stealing in my book." he nods, "Second, the guy's wallet was lying empty on the floor."

"She took his credit cards?"

"No, she's smarter than that." He pulls a wallet out of his jacket pocket, "But no cash. She took it."

"How do you know he had cash, people don't

carry cash." Grey thinks about it for a minute. "And why do you have the wallet?"

"Every guy at a strip club carries cash. You can't slide your card in a tart's gash and get a lap dance. He had none in his pockets and none in his wallet." Angus slides the wallet back into his jacket. "I'd hate to see how they'd handle the new chip cards."

Grey blows out a disgusted breath, "You haven't answered my second question, why you have the wallet." Grey glowers at Angus.

"Because I do know how to use the credit cards," Angus says. "The Bubblegum Factory is on the left."

Grey surveys the outside of the club, repulsed at the dilapidated building. He sniffs at the air hoping to catch her scent, but all he smells is the rancid humans, the worst kind.

As they walk through the door, Grey notices a flock of women around a man. "Is that him?"

"How'd you guess?" Angus asks.

"Because unless he's got a hell of a lot of charisma or money, he'd not draw that kind of crowd unless he's a vampire." Grey's control is slipping fast, and he's too distracted by the naked women to be disgusted. He wants to fuck every last one of them. A wave of jealousy comes over him that this young vampire has all their attention.

"Grey?" Angus questions trailing behind. "You've got that look again."

"I'm fine." Grey balls his fists at his sides.

They reach the group of women and sitting at the center is another vampire. "Michael?" Grey inquires.

"Who wants to know?" The vamp answers flippantly, without looking away from one of the women.

"Michael," Angus says with warning. "We're here to help you."

Michael looks up and in a split second darts from his chair toward the door.

Grey easily reaches the door long before Michael, blocking his way. "No, you're coming with us."

The inexperienced vampire has little control over his enhanced movements. He's no match for an ancient vampire.

"You don't know what you're dealing with, you'd be smart to mind your own business," Michael warns.

Grey balls Michael's t-shirt in his fists and lifts him up, "Listen to me you little shit. I don't want to be in this dump, cleaning up Charles' mess, but I don't give a flying fuck whether I kill you here or get you to the Company House. The choice is yours."

Michael's eyes widen, and the bouncers in the club start to close in on them. His eyes shift wildly. "But I'm hungry."

"Grey, take him, let's go," Angus says nervously.

Grey looks around, he's thirsty and ready for a fight. Without a word, he dashes out of the club with Michael in tow. He gets in the car and drives off without Angus.

Michael sits slightly dazed in the passenger seat, "Where are you taking me?"

"Where Charles should have taken you, to begin with. They will help you acclimate." Grey says looking straight ahead. He can only focus on dropping Michael off and getting back on the hunt for his Bloodmate.

"I'm hungry," Michael complains. "This sucks, I have all this power, and you're going to take me somewhere that they're going to lock me up? Give me cold blood? Fuck that."

Grey can no longer contain his anger, "Shut up."

Michael opens the car door and tries to jump out while it's still moving. Grey grabs him and pulls the car to the side of the road. He gets out and yanks Michael from the car by the neck. His grip tightens, and he's working hard to not snap his head right off. "I don't care what happens to you. At this point, I'd like to kill you myself. Apparently, Charles did not teach you the discretion necessary for our kind. If you've been killing, that causes problems for all of us, but if I kill you, it solves all of our problems. I have no patience for your bullshit. So your choices are, get in the car, be quiet and behave yourself, or I can end you now and get on with my life."

Michael is unable to speak with Grey's hand

wrapped around his neck. Grey says lowering his eyes to Michael's, "You can nod yes if you want to live."

Michael trembles in Grey's hold and nods his head once. Grey throws him in the car and resumes his course.

Chapter Ten

Mila bursts through the door startling Hera, "We have to go." She looks around the empty suite and begins going from room to room looking for Hera. "Hera!"

Hera comes in the front door of the suite rolling a room service cart. "What's with all the yelling?"

"What the heaven is that?" Mila motions to the cart.

"Room service," Hera says it like it's obvious.

"How did you get room service?" Mila's amazed by her friend's constant resourcefulness.

"Easy, I phase into another room where the occupant is gone and order food." Hera lifts the cover off one of the plates, "Fruit?"

"No." Mila looks around the room at three other carts with leftover food. "Been hungry?"

"Not for long. The food is delicious here." Hera pumps her brow.

"Nevermind that." Mila resets herself, "We have to go."

Hera barely moves, "Why?"

Mila balls her fists at her side, she knows there's more to what she's feeling than just the panic of Elomere finding her, but she can't put her finger on it and definitely doesn't have the patience for Hera right now. "Because we have to, please just get your stuff together."

"Is this because of the Vampire and his creepy brownie?"

Mila freezes in place, "Vampire?"

"Yeah, the vamp was hot as hell with this british accent that was just..." Hera licks her lips thinking about him.

Mila loses control grabbing her friend by the wrist, "Get your dirty little mind off of him."

"Oh, so you do know who I'm talking about." Hera pulls her lips to the side.

Mila lets out a groan, "I didn't know, I don't know. We just have to go."

"You're not making sense." Hera widens her eyes.

"I know. I'm not making sense to myself. I'm so hungry...for blood and..." Mila trails off.

"And what?" Hera's intrigued.

"It doesn't matter. We're leaving." Mila get serious again.

"But it's so comfortable here." Hera whines. "Are we going back under?"

"No, I'm not ready to give up." Mila insists as she hurries to the bedroom to pack her small bag.

"Fine," Hera packs her things, and they meet in the living room. "Okay, where to and how are we getting there."

"I was thinking we could take a bus, maybe go south." Mila pulls an old paper map out of her backpack and studies it.

"Is it warm there?" Hera asks, "Because I don't do well in the cold."

"I think so." Mila continues to look at the map.

"I'm telling you, we really should get one of those phone things that everyone has here. All the information you could ever need, right at your fingertips. It's amazing." Hera says, excited at the thought. "If we got two, we could communicate instantly."

"You seem to be getting quite comfortable here." Mila remarks.

"I could live here for a while." She shrugs. "I'm sure I'll survive for as long as it takes for you to find your mother."

"I would love if you stayed longer." Mila hangs her head relaxing her shoulders. "I just hate the thought of being alone."

"I know. Take your time to decide if you want to stay or not. I'll stick with you at least until then." Hera laughs.

"I appreciate it. You coming with me and being able to get me back made the decision to leave a lot easier." Mila puts her bag down. "The thought of leaving my father still saddens me, but knowing that for now, as long as you're with me, I can go back goes a long way."

"Your mother was one of my dearest friends, and I know she wanted you to be happy above all else." Hera eyes the plate of fruit and grabs a bunch of grapes. "Did you want some?"

"No, I just want to go." Mila swallows hard, feeling an intense hunger, but it's not for food. It's for that Vampire. When she phased back in at the club, he was gone. Nothing left but the scent of him.

She didn't get a chance to really hear him speak, she was so terrified when she'd been caught that she phased out. The thought of his accent dances in her mind. She shakes her head, *focus, Mila.*

A Vampire's Thirst

Chapter Eleven

Grey had not anticipated rush hour traffic in downtown Atlanta. The sky is beginning to lighten, and the clock is ticking. There's a time bomb sitting in his front seat and another sitting in his mind. He has to get to her, now.

If he doesn't get Michael to the safe house soon, he's going to leave a horrible mess in the front of his Bentley. Grey can walk in the sun, but a young vampire like Michael won't last a minute.

He glances at the sidewalk, there's only a few

people straggling by. Apparently, no one walks in Atlanta anymore.

Michael glances in Grey's direction, he's starting to tremble. "Hey, I don't mean to be a pain, but the sun's coming up. Is it much further?"

Grey knows they're in trouble, it's not going to end well. He doesn't answer Michael evaluating if it's safe for him to just go on foot.

He can't leave Michael on the side of the road to explode in a bloody mess, and he can't just leave his car in the middle of the road unmanned. He's caught between a rock and a hard place. They've already sat for two cycles at a traffic light and have at least two to go.

He considers popping up onto the curb, but that would draw too much attention. He can't pull off the road until he gets through this light, then there's a place for him to leave the car.

"Angus!" Grey yells out giving Michael a start.

"What about him?" Michael says shrinking in his seat.

Grey picks up the phone and dials, "Angus."

"What happened to you?" Angus says in a hushed tone.

"I had to get Michael out of there, but now I'm stuck in traffic." Grey's tone is riddled with panic.

"Shit." Angus hisses.

"Shit is right. The sun's coming up." Grey says.

"Double shit," Angus says. "Can you leave the car?"

"Yes, I can, but I need you to meet me at the safe house. I don't want to be stuck there talking to anyone. I need to go find her." Grey says.

"That's the thing. I've found her." Angus says.

"What?" Grey yells, "Stay away from her."

"Calm down, I'm outside their hotel room, and I can still hear them in there," Angus says with excitement at his achievement. "I figured you were taking Michael to the safe house, and I should follow up on the girl."

"Don't you dare touch her." Grey threatens.

"I have no intention, but we've got a blood fairy here, and that's a real problem for my city. I need to make sure she stays put--"

"You're turning her in?" Grey's blood boils with rage, "I'll rip every rancid vein from your body one by one."

"Calm down. I'm not turning her in. I was keeping tabs on her until you got here." Angus is exasperated. "You know, you've never been so irrational before."

"I'm sorry," Grey says breathing a sigh of relief. "It's the Thirst."

"It's okay." Angus says, "Do you want me to meet you at the safe house or stay here?"

There's a long stretch of silence while Grey considers the options. "Stay put, don't let her go anywhere and don't let anyone near her."

"You got it. I'll stay here, you get Michael to the safe house and make sure you talk to Barb. Charles has already made arrangements for Michael."

"Yeah, I'm sure the kind of arrangements that keeps him out of hot water for a rogue youngling." Grey disconnects the call and glances at Michael with an air of pity. "You're going to be okay. You just have to learn control and understand the rules."

Michael eyes the horizon nervously, "It may not be something I have to worry about."

"I'm going to get you there. Trust me." Grey says pulling into the parking lot. He gets out and with his super speed picks Michael up out of the car, throws him over his shoulder and heads for the safe house.

He gives no thought to humans seeing him, the danger doesn't concern him. There's an element of empathy that's managed to break through the madness of the Thirst. He has to get Michael to the safe house before he dies. He focuses all of his energy on that one task. Then he can move on to the next.

Grey dodges the few humans on the street, leaving a brisk wind in his wake. People turn and stare, trying to capture the streak on their phones. He leaps over a car pulling out from a side street.

"I think I'm going to be sick." Michael presses out.

"Do not throw up on me." Grey grinds out, "This

is an Armani suit and probably cost more than any dwelling you've ever lived in."

The sun creeps over the horizon and Grey can smell Michael's burning flesh. Michael begins to cry out in pain. Grey pushes forward harder, praying he can beat the sun to the door of the safe house.

He whizzes up the front steps and breaks through the front door whisking Michael straight to the darkroom in the basement.

"What in the blazes?" A proper woman with her hair in a tight bun calls out from the front hall.

Grey makes his way back upstairs adjusting his suit. "Miss Barb." He tips his head taking her hand and kissing it.

"Well, if it isn't Grey Hart, here in the flesh." She purses her lips, "I suppose you just deposited Charles' little problem in the darkroom?"

"Yes, and he's in rough shape. I got him here as soon as possible, but we didn't quite beat the sun. He's going to need a lot of blood." Grey warns.

"Oh Lord, it figures." She inhales a deep breath,

"Tasha, we have an emergency in the dark room."

A slender young woman comes from the kitchen with a handful of towels and large bag. "I've got it Miss Barb."

"Here, let me take that, please show Mr. Hart out." Miss Barb takes the items from Tasha and warns, "Mr. Hart can charm the dew off a honeysuckle, just see him out and come downstairs. I'm going to need your help." She finishes with a scolding look in Grey's direction.

"Thank you, Miss Barb." Grey smiles and heads for the door, "I can see myself out, please take care of Michael."

"We will, and you take care of yourself." She disappears down the stairs and Grey steps outside the house.

He opens his Lyft app to see how close a driver is. He can withstand the sun but has the feeling he's going to need all of his strength for what's coming next.

A Vampire's Thirst

Chapter Twelve

Mila peeks out the peephole in the door. "Shit." She turns around.

"What's wrong?" Hera asks standing behind her laden with bags.

Mila eyes her luggage, "Seriously? Do you actually have more stuff? I told you we needed to travel light."

Hera huffs out, "I didn't know how long I'd be gone and I've picked up a few essentials."

"This is going to be impossible." Mila walks away from the door defeated.

"Why?" Hera looks out the peephole. "The Brownie. This is easy, all we have to do is toss a coin down the corridor, and he's no longer a problem."

"That's not going to work," Mila says looking out the peephole again. "The elevators are close, but if it isn't on our floor, we could end up falling down the shaft if we phase in there." She starts to think.

Hera puts her bags down, "You're making this so much harder than it has to be."

"What are you going to do?" Mila asks in a panic and blocks Hera's way to the door.

"I'm going to drain him, and then we walk out." She tries to get past Mila.

"No, we can't do that. He hasn't done anything wrong." Mila protests.

"Neither did any of the men you robbed at the strip clubs." Hera rolls her eyes, "I don't see how this would be different, other than I promise you that Brownie doesn't have so much as a coin on him."

"The men in the strip club were different. They

were...disgusting and happy to use women for their own repulsive urges." Mila's confused that the thought both makes her ill and hot all at once. "I have got to get a grip on myself."

Hera looks out the peephole, "Okay, so let's just slide a dollar bill under the door and when he comes to get it, we knock him out. He'll be fine, we don't do any permanent damage."

Mila lets out an exasperated breath and pushes Hera out of the way to study the emergency escape route on the door. "Here's what we do," She presses her finger on the map, "We phase into the adjoining rooms until we reach the stairwell. Then we're out of here, he doesn't see us, doesn't get hurt, and all is well."

"What about the vamp?" Hera points out. "We don't know where he is. He could be in the stairwell."

"No, I don't think so." She remembers the spark she felt at the club when he was there.

"Okay, so that's what you want to do, you want to phase from room to room until we get to the stairwell, with all of our bags and then hustle down the stairs." Hera laughs, "You're ridiculous."

"I'm ridiculous? You're the one that brought half the underworld in your suitcases." Mila motions to the bags walking away in a huff. "And your *essentials*. Do you have any better ideas?"

"Yeah, slip a dollar under the door and knock him out." She peeks out the door.

"You know, Brownies have very good ears," Angus calls from outside the door.

Mila and Hera freeze in place staring at each other. Hera looks at the door, "What do we do?"

"Let me in. I don't mean you any harm."

"We're not letting you in." Mila calls out nervously then stands in front of Hera, "Seriously, what do we do?"

Hera holds up a finger and widens her eyes conveying a message. She goes to the desk in the main room and picks up a pen and paper and starts jotting something down. "Maybe we should just let him in."

"Are you mad?" Mila says before reading the note.

Hera rattles the paper in front of Mila's face, "Read."

You phase out of here. We'll meet up at the emergency spot.

Mila nods her head knowingly. "I don't think it's safe to let him in, but we've got to get out of here." She plays along.

"What do you want with us?" Hera calls out the door.

"Nothing really, I was sent here to keep you safe," Angus says tugging proudly at the lapel of his brown jacket.

Hera giggles, "*You're* going to keep us safe?"

"Yes. My friend, Grey. He needs to speak with you. He can help you." Angus sounds pretty convincing.

Hera scrawls something on the pad,

Go, I'll meet up with you in an hour.

Mila takes the pen and paper.

How will you get out?

Hera rolls her eyes, "Trust me, I've handled far worse in my time."

"Not worse than The Directive," Angus answers thinking Hera's speaking to him.

Hera waves Mila off, "I'm not worried about The Directive."

Mila phases out into the next hotel room, then the next. Two more times and she looks out the peephole with a clear view of the door to the stairwell.

Fear and exhilaration fills her. She doesn't know if it's safe if there's someone there. The brownie likely heard their plan. She paces for a moment and hears stirring in the room. The occupant is waking up.

With no other choice, she closes her eyes and phases into the stairwell. She inhales a scent that stops her in her tracks. She wants to follow it, there's something magnetic about it. The sound of a door slamming startles her out of her dreamlike state. She peeks over the railing of the stairs and sees someone coming up the stairs. She phases down two floors past whoever it is and gets on the elevator on the next floor.

A Vampire's Thirst

Chapter Thirteen

"Angus! Where is she?" Grey can smell her scent heavy in the air. It's driving him beyond madness.

"She's in here. I did just as you said, no one in, no one out." Angus nods proudly.

Grey pushes past him throwing the door open, nearly ripping it off the hinges.

He sees the woman from before standing in the middle of the room with three large suitcases all around her, with a snarky smile she asks, "Are you my ride?"

"Where is she? I have to find her?" Grey frantically stalks through the suite.

"She's gone," Hera says showing no fear.

"I have to find her." Grey says desperately.

"You won't." Hera smiles sweetly.

"I will find her, and you're going to help me." Grey insists doing everything in his power to not lose the last of his control.

"Nope." Hera shrugs.

Grey fills with rage and starts toward Hera.

Hera lifts her arms and Grey freezes in place, "Listen vampire, I forgave you for disturbing me earlier, but you're going to have to leave her alone."

Grey bucks against the invisible binds yelling in a crazed tone, "I have to find her. I love her!"

"You don't know what you're dealing with here. I'm older, smarter and more powerful than you could wish to be." Hera gets directly in front of Grey and leans into him, "You're out of your league."

Angus struggles in his binds, "He doesn't want to hurt her."

"How could you possibly love her, you don't even

know her name." Hera laughs, "You're a fool, she's not going to be in this realm much longer anyway."

"What do you mean?" Grey asks as a streak of pain shoots through him at the thought of never being with her.

"She's here on a wild goose chase to find her mother," Hera says with a lilt of sadness in her tone. "But honestly, I doubt we'll ever find her, even if she is still alive."

"I can help." Grey pleads, "But I have to find..." Grey searches his mind trying to think of her name, something pops into his mind, and a smile stretches across his lips, "I have to find Mila."

Hera glances between Grey and Angus. "How did you know her name?"

"I just did," Grey says still pleading not letting on that he heard it earlier. "She's my Bloodmate."

Hera rolls her eyes, "That's not possible."

"It *is* possible," Grey says hanging his head. "There was a part of me that thought it was just a myth, but what I feel for her is very real. I haven't met her, but I just know, she's my Bloodmate."

"Well, that would complicate things quite a bit," Hera says still not releasing the men.

"How?"

"Even if I did believe you, there's no way for you to be together. She has to go back to the Underworld, she can't stay here forever." Hera pulls her lips to the side.

"I'll go with her. I don't care, I have to be with her." Madness creeps in, and Grey can feel that he's losing himself.

"You're just a crazy vampire. I've seen your kind before, thinking love is the only way that you'll feel life again." Hera waves her hand pacing toward the window. "We would never allow a filthy vamp in the Underworld, that's why they go somewhere else when they cease to exist."

"I had a very fulfilled life, or so I thought." Grey laments.

"Honestly, mum, Grey here is one of the most balanced vamps I've ever met. The way she drives him nuts, I believe this whole Bloodmate problem he's having." Angus says looking at Grey with sadness. "The poor sod hadn't had a live donor in a hundred years, and then yesterday, he couldn't stop himself."

"Maybe he was just hungry." Hera dismisses Angus' words.

"Or maybe he's in love." Angus offers, "There's only one way to find out."

Hera seems to be giving what they're saying a lot of thought. She turns around, "Well, I wish you the best of luck." She piles her smaller bag on top of one of the suitcases with wheels.

"Hey, what are you doing?" Angus asks.

"Leaving," Hera says strutting toward the door.

The last of Grey's hope leaves his being, "When you see her, tell her I'll find her."

"I'll tell her no such thing, I'll be taking her home today." Hera turns the corner in the corridor.

"She was stalling the whole time," Angus says still unable to move.

"Just figuring that out now, genius?" Grey says.

"So now what do we do?" Angus struggles.

"We wait for the spell to wear off." Grey seems to

have given up.

"How long will that take?" Angus asks.

"Probably as long as it will take her to get to Mila and get her far away from here." Grey's hope is waning. The madness will take him over soon, and he fears he will be lost forever.

Chapter Fourteen

Mila paces the sidewalk in Underground Atlanta. *Where the hell is Hera?* She thinks hoping that she was able to get away.

The shops are beginning to open, and she feels an intense hunger panging against the pit of her belly. The feeling subsides when she thinks of the vampire, there was something soothing in his eyes.

Their eyes met for only a split second, but it's burned in her memory forever. There was something eternal in that moment, and she needs to be near him. Curl into his form and stay there forever in the comfort of him.

*Mila, what's wrong with you? You don't know anything about him, other than that he was looking for her and he's a vampire.*She scolds her wandering thoughts.

A protective wave comes over her, she knows how dangerous it would be for him to even know her. Anger flares inside her knowing what Elomere would do to him, what The Directive would do to him if they found her with him. She's heard stories her whole life about the evil Directive.

"Together?" She says out loud mocking herself for sounding crazy, she doesn't know him or anything about him. Except what she felt in that moment.

"Can I help you?" A old man steps down the stairs of one of the shops carrying a sign.

Mila startles, "Oh, um, no, I'm just waiting for someone."

"Okay," The gentleman smiles and props the sign up. "I have a fresh batch of croissants, just out of the oven."

Mila slides her hand into her pocket feeling the

wad of cash and considers her growling stomach, "That sounds lovely."

The shopkeeper waves her inside, "I thought you looked hungry."

Mila can smell his blood pumping through him thinking that's what she really wants. Her body tenses, knowing she can't take his blood. It's too risky. "You have no idea."

"I might." He says going behind the counter. "Would you like anything on it?"

Mila looks around the bakery in wonder at all the delightful goodies in the glass cases. "Everything looks so delicious."

"Thank you." He smiles. "Butter? Cream cheese?"

"No thank you." Mila says, "Just the croissant." She pulls a five dollar bill from her pocket and reaches across the counter.

"No, this is on the house, I've always been a sucker for a pretty girl." He says handing her the pastry in a small brown bag. "If you need anything else, let me know."

She can't help but think, *a pint of your blood would*

be lovely. But she nods and walks quickly out of the shop.

When she reaches the sidewalk the sound of his heart beating blood through his veins floods her senses, she needs it.

"Mila." Hera's voice brings Mila out of her blood trance.

"Oh, thank goodness." Mila breathes a sigh of relief.

"What's wrong with you? You're sweating." Hera asks patting Mila's forehead.

"All I can think of is draining every human. I'm so hungry." She says feeling embarrassed.

"Well then, I guess it's a good thing we're leaving." Hera motions for Mila to follow her.

"The bus stations' this way." Mila points in the opposite direction.

"We're not taking the bus," Hera says with authority.

"But if we use the portals, they'll be able to track us down." Mila protests.

Hera stops in place and takes Mila's cheeks in her

hands, "Sweetheart, I know you wanted to find your mother. But it's getting too dangerous."

Mila steps out of her grasp, "What?" She studies Hera for a moment, "I'm not going home. Not now, maybe not ever."

"You don't have a choice. The Directive knows you're here, if they catch you they won't send you home, they'll end you." Hera explains.

"I'd rather be dead than go back home." Mila's heart shatters into a million pieces thinking of being in a different realm than the vampire. "I don't understand what the big deal is anyway. My mother's here."

"We don't know where your mother is, or if she's alive. But we do know *we're* not supposed to be here." Hera says walking toward the place where she can conjure the portal.

"You never had any intention of helping me, did you?" Mila makes the realization.

"I do want to help you, but now that we've been discovered, we have to go." Hera walks back toward Mila taking her by the wrist.

"No." Mila holds her ground.

"Stop behaving like a spoiled child. You're going home. I'm sorry things aren't ideal for you there, but maybe your father will reconsider knowing how serious you are about not being bound to Elomere." Hera offers.

"I doubt it." Mila hangs her head. "Besides, what I want is here. That vampire, I can't stop thinking about him."

Hera ticks her head back, "The vampire?"

"Yeah, he was at the club. He thought he was rescuing me." Mila laughs.

Hera's expression turns serious, "What did this vampire look like?"

Mila goes starry-eyed, "He was incredibly handsome with dirty blonde spiky hair, strong wide shoulders and incredible blue eyes. His jaw was pleasantly rugged, and his lips were full and kissable..."

"Good grief." Hera throws her head back. "You spent a sum total of what, three seconds in his presence."

"That's all it took." Mila puts her hand over her stomach.

"What's wrong?" Hera asks with concern.

"I'm hungry." Mila's starry-eyed expression turns quickly to bloodlust. She eyes the few people filing their way into Underground Atlanta. "I need to feed."

"No, you do not need to feed. Not here." Hera takes her wrist more forcefully, "We're going now before this gets even worse. You can feed on Ty when you get home."

"No." Mila's eyes begin to take on the tell-tale red hue when the bloodlust takes over her kind.

"Mila, do *not* do this. We have to go, the sooner, the better. Please don't make me --"

"You're supposed to be my friend!" Mila jerks her wrist away, "You're supposed to be helping me and all you're trying to do is take me back to where I'm going to be miserable."

"I'm not your friend, I'm your caretaker. I've been your caretaker since you were born and your mother ran off. I'm going to do what I've done your whole life and make the best decision for you when you aren't capable." Hera's words burn hard on Mila's heart.

"What?" She breathes out on a whisper, her being floods with anger at the thought.

"Mila, you've always been a dreamer entertaining thoughts of finding your mother and living here, in the light above the realm. You don't belong here, you aren't welcome here. Your father figured you'd realize that when you spent a few days here and I was to bring you back. It's for the best." There's a hint of pain in Hera's voice.

Mila's emotions are running away with her. Betrayal, hunger, sadness, defeat all mingle inside her heart. "You're just another one of my father's hired goons." Mila shakes her head.

Hera takes two tentative steps toward her, "Honey, I love you. It's not like that, but it's been my role in your life to lead you toward what's best."

"Liar." Mila cries out and phases away from Hera.

Chapter Fifteen

Grey struggles harder against the spell. He has to get out of this now. He pools all of his energy, flexing every last one of his muscles. He growls out a loud roar and pushes against the invisible binds. With a flash, the spell is lifted.

Angus collapses to the floor. "Oh thank the heavens."

Grey frantically looks around the room for any clue as to where they went. He has to get to her before she's gone forever. His mind races with thoughts of how to get to the underworld. It's forbidden to go there, "Angus, do you know anyone that can get me to the underworld?"

"Oh, *that's* not a good idea," Angus warns.

"If we can't find her here, I'll go anywhere, do anything to find her. I'm going to go mad without her." Grey paces the room.

"Let's try to figure out where they went." Angus looks around the room. "I don't know anyone that can get you to the Underworld, not alive anyway."

"I don't care if I have to die to get there." Grey grinds it out. "I have to be with her."

Angus blows out a breath, "But there's no guarantee --"

"I don't give a fuck, I have to find her." Grey bellows and Angus is taken aback.

"Okay, okay. Let's find her." Angus sifts through the tourist pamphlets on the table. "Hey, look at this."

"What." Grey snaps at him.

"Terminus." Angus nods with wide eyes, "I bet this is where they are."

"Why there?" Grey asks snatching the pamphlet.

"Because that battleax wants to get her home. There's probably a portal point she can open at Terminus. There are rumors that they used to keep it guarded." Angus starts for the door. "Come on, it's the best we've got."

"You're right. Let's go." Grey hurries out the door. He turns toward Angus, "Meet me there."

"We should really stick together," Angus warns.

"No time. You can't keep --"

"No, you can't be seen using your vampire speed. It's ten in the morning. The streets are full of people. You have to use prudence." Angus tries to reason with Grey.

"I don't care." Grey's jaw is tense and popping.

"You should." Vash's voice comes from the stairwell.

Shit. Grey thinks to himself. "Listen, I have to go."

"Grey, I've been patient, I've not brought the home office in, but you're leaving me with no choice. You're little stunt this morning is all over the internet." Vash tisks.

"I solved that problem for you. Michael is tucked away at the Company safe house." Grey points out.

"That does not solve my problems." Vash shakes his head. "We found three more bodies, one of them was still warm. It couldn't have been the young vamp."

Grey blows out a breath, "Can you be sure?"

"Yes, absolutely sure." Vash affirms, "We got a report from Underground, one of the shopkeepers was found dead behind his counter, drained. An eyewitness saw your blood fairy there."

"No, God no. She's got the Thirst. I have to get to her." Grey starts for the hallway.

"We have to bring her in," Vash calls after him. "I've already contacted Clarence."

Grey can't hear him, he has to get to Mila before anyone else does.

All he felt from her is kindness, sweetness and the thought of this Thirst making her do bad things kills him. He races down the stairwell and slows to a brisk human pace when reaches the lobby.

He crosses the street and stays on the sidewalk,

trying to avoid the direct sunlight. He looks around at the people on the street wanting desperately to go faster, but there aren't enough back alleys for him to walk through without being seen.

After walking for five minutes, he has about another seven minutes left before he reaches Underground Atlanta at a human pace.

"Fuck this." He grinds out and uses his vampire speed to get to Underground in a minute. He slows his speed once down the stairs. He searches for other supernaturals, likely here looking for Mila.

Grey straightens his suit and walks slowly through the darkened cobblestone pathways. His Thirst is undeniable and dangerous. He wants to drain every human that walks by him. He keeps his head down as he passes a bakery with three werewolves standing outside the entrance. The sign in the window says "Closed".

"Try not to look so much like a vampire," Angus says coming up beside him.

"How the hell did you get here so fast?" Grey asks.

"I'm a brownie, I have my ways." Angus waves his

arms around. “Besides, I knew I had to get here to keep you from doing anything stupid.”

“That’s a switch.” Grey widens his eyes.

“True statement, old friend.” Angus nods, “Now, less like a vampire.”

“How do I look less like a vampire?” Grey says while continuing down the sidewalk.

“less arrogant. That’s a start.”

“I am not arrogant.” Grey insists.

“Yeah, okay so this is a lost cause.” Angus rolls his eyes, “Any idea where she is, or if she’s still here?”

Grey gives his answer consideration. He’s known Angus for a long time, he knows that Angus’ loyalty is always hinged on self-preservation. “I don’t think she’s here anymore, I have no idea where she could be.”

“Okay, so we do a quick sweep here and then where to?” He asks.

“She could be anywhere, and with the easy access to MARTA, she could have hopped on the train and be anywhere by now.” Grey pinches the bridge of his nose. “Let’s split up, you check here in the mall area, I'm going to look in Kenny's Alley."

"Okay," Angus hesitates. "Be careful."

"You do the same and if you find her, call me immediately," Grey says in a severe tone.

"Sure thing." Angus heads in the opposite direction from Grey.

Grey feels a an undeniable draw to Kenny's Alley, it would be much less populated during the day. He enters the area where the bars are open at night. He feels her presence and her fear. She's hiding here somewhere.

He stalks toward her scent, his pace certain as he approaches an alley toward the back she steps out from the shadow and stands completely still.

He's torn between going to her and taking her, making her his and taking all of her in. He pauses for a moment and just gazes upon her beauty. Her long black hair, azure eyes and lips full of desire. He can't remain still for one more moment.

He goes to her and takes her into his arms, "Mila."

She surrenders to him, allowing her body to melt

into his embrace, "Grey," she breathes into his ear. "What took you so long?"

"I'm here now." He gazes into her eyes running his thumb across her alabaster cheek and crashes his lips over hers.

He slowly explores all parts of her mouth, tasting her, trying not to be too hungry and frantic to take all of her in. He feels her surrender, the world around them disappears, and in this moment Grey feels alive for the first time in centuries. His heart pounds wildly in his chest and cock ticks to life being so close to her. He pauses, breathless, "I want you."

"I'm yours." She gasps before wrapping her hand around the back of his neck and pulling him in for another epic kiss.

They are lost in this moment, relief at finally being together spirals through them heating the air around them with incredible passion.

"Grey!" Angus yells from across the alley.

Grey goes on alert and catches the scent of werewolves nearby. "Directive, we've got to go."

"Elomere." Mila's worried tone catches in her throat. "Let's go!" She wraps her arms around Grey, closes her eyes and phases out.

Chapter Sixteen

They phase in at street level. Grey is astonished and slightly confused, "How did we get here." Mila looks around in a panic, "I'll explain later, which way do we go?"

"Come with me." Grey takes her hand, "I'm going to get you out of here."

They start down the busy street riddled with tourists and mothers on a stroll with their little ones. Grey curses at the number of people around. He wants to use his speed, but there are too many witnesses. He's already in hot water for his stunt this morning with Michael, and if he's got any chance at all at saving Mila and keeping her here, he has to behave. Right now, though, he has to keep her safe.

They weave in and out of the crowd. Every chance he gets he steals a glance in her direction, he can't stop looking at her, marveling at her incredible beauty.

She glances up at him with a demure smile.

Grey pushes aside his desire to take her into his arms and take her right here. His drive to be with her is only getting stronger, he was hoping that once he found her, he'd be able to think clearer. His need for blood and sex is becoming more compelling, and his concentration is waning.

"Where are we going?" Mila asks slightly out of breath.

Grey really doesn't know, he's heading away from the perceived danger. He doesn't want to tell her, but he needs to get her to safety. He's not sure how long Angus can stall Vash and his pack.

A memory of this morning pops into his head, "My car."

"Your car?" She asks confused. "Where is it?"

"Not far from here, I left it in a parking lot this morning." Grey changes direction and heads for the lot.

"Shit." Mila hisses looking behind them.

"What is it?" Grey asks maintaining his focus on moving forward.

"They're coming!" Mila's voice quivers with fear.

"We're almost there." Grey tries to reassure her.

They reach his car, and he opens the door for her, "Get in."

Mila climbs into the front seat, Grey hands her the keys, "Lock it and don't open it for anyone but me."

"They can smash the windows." Her eyes are wide and full of panic. It sends a shock of anger through Grey seeing his woman afraid.

"They will have a very difficult time breaking through *these* windows," Grey says in a calm tone.

Mila looks unsure. Grey puts his hand on her shoulder, "Do you trust me?"

"Yes." Mila nods. "How do I lock it?"

"Press that button." Grey points to the lock button on the keyfob and closes the door as Vash, and his pack of four werewolves reaches them.

"Gentlemen." Grey nods coolly fighting to maintain his composure. The bloodlust and rage running through him at the thought of Mila being in danger is proving difficult to cope with.

"Grey, what do you think you're doing?" Vash asks walking slowly toward him.

"I'm getting her to safety." Grey answers.

"She can't be here, it's forbidden. We have to bring her in." Vash says calmly.

Grey maintains his awareness of the wolves flanking him, he eyes each of them making a game plan in his head of how he will kill every last one of them to protect Mila. "I'm afraid that's not possible."

"That's not wise." Vash lowers his tone to emphasise the threat, "She *is* coming with us."

"It's you who is being unwise. I will deal with The Directive in respect to Mila. You should leave it at that." Grey lifts his head and continues to watch the wolves closing in.

"You know I can't do that."

"But you will." A sly smile dances on Grey's lips, "You see, we are in full view of a very busy street. If you do not let me go and take her to safety, I will destroy you and your cronies right here, full vampire style. The only way you'd have any chance of survival would be if you all shifted, and even then I will decimate every last one of you."

Vash surveys the area, a look of realization comes over him, "You know you're going to have to answer for this."

"I'm sure," Grey affirms.

"And she's going to have to answer for the murders and the treaty she's breaking by being here." Vash's expression softens, and he takes a step toward Grey, "The best you can do for her right now is to get her back to the Underworld. It's the only place she'll be safe from The

Directive." Vash looks down and away, "You, on the other hand...are screwed."

"I'll handle The Directive." Grey takes his queue and walks to the driver's side of the car. His thumbprint opens the door.

"Or they'll handle you," Vash says as he and his men back away.

"What did they say?" Mila asks wide-eyed.

"They said everything's fine." Grey answers pushing the button starting the car.

"Lying to me is not a good way to start things." Mila pins him with a serious look.

"We've got some issues to work out, but it will be okay." Grey puts his hand on her thigh. "Right now, my goal is to get you somewhere safe."

He doesn't finish the thought out loud, all he can think about is being inside her, tasting every part of her and making her his.

Mila puts her hand on Grey's, "Why are you doing this? Risking yourself for me?"

"Because you're mine." Grey smiles pulling out of the parking lot.

"Whoa, hold on a minute." Mila gets riled up.

"And I am yours." He says.

"I don't understand." She says shaking her head.

"You knew my name. You knew me before we ever touched." Grey says.

Mila sits in silent contemplation for a moment, her lips part and with astonishment, "Yes, I did...how?"

"We are Bloodmates," Grey says with a nod.

"I don't know what that means." Mila studies his expression.

"It means that long before either of us were created, we were meant to be together. The feelings you're having of lust and hunger...that's the Thirst created when you come close to your Bloodmate before you consummate." He explains.

Mila's cheeks flush, and she squirms in her seat, "Oh. I-I thought it was the effect of being here, topside."

"You feel it." He says with a growl squeezing her thigh.

"Oh yes, I feel it." Mila's breath becomes labored and she's resisting the urge to climb on him now. She reaches over running her hand up his thigh and wraps her hand around the form of his hard cock. "I feel it." She moans.

Grey swallows hard and releases a breath. "We have to get to safety first."

"This looks pretty safe." Mila leans over running her lips along his ear. "I need you." She growls out.

"I need you too. But we have to get far from here."

"Now." Mila insists nibbling his neck.

"Holy hell." Grey groans. "No. Just hold on a little longer."

"I don't think I can." Her breath is needy on his neck.

"I was talking to myself." Grey huffs a laugh. "I have to stop at the hotel, and we'll get out of town. Then we can..."

"Fuck," Mila growls running her hands along the plain of his chest.

"Everything." Grey rolls his eyes trying to maintain his focus. But all he can think about is being inside of her.

He slides his hand up her thigh to the warmth between her legs. He pushes her panties aside, sliding two fingers inside her pussy.

Mila stills for a moment gasping for air, "I can't..."

Grey gently strokes her sliding in and out with purpose resting his thumb on the bundle of nerves piquing her excitement. He sees the hotel coming into view, slides his hand out leaving her feeling cold and empty.

He looks into her eyes, "Soon my love." He slips his fingers into his mouth slowly to savor her essence. "Soon."

His cock is raging, taking over all reason and sense. Grey can't control it much longer, there's nothing left in him to hold him back from feasting on her pussy.

They pull into the valet of the hotel, William opens the door for Mila taking her hand to help her from the car. Grey wants to snap his neck for touching her. He comes around the side of the car and suppresses a growl as he takes Mila's hand from the valet.

"Professor Hart." The valet greets him.

Grey says through gritted teeth. "Keep it up front, I'll be leaving shortly."

"Yes, sir," William says in a curious tone.

Mila and Grey walk briskly through the lobby to the stairwell. He scoops her up cleaving her to his chest and uses his vampire speed up the stairs to the penthouse level. They get to the door, and he reaches into his pocket looking for his keycard.

Impatient, Mila wraps her arms around him and phases them inside the room. She looks up at him through hooded eyes, "I couldn't wait."

"You are amazing?" Grey smiles running his finger down her arm.

"So are you." She says raising a brow feeling his hard chest beneath her fingers.

"I want to know everything about --"

Mila puts her finger over his lips shushing him, "Later, it doesn't matter right now."

He lets out a breath and slides his hand behind her neck pulling her lips to his. When they connect everything stills and speeds up at the same time. The world around them melts to a colorful palette of shadows and shapes that are insignificant.

His tongue invades her mouth and dances with hers as fire explodes in every part of him. For hundreds of years since he was turned he wondered if he had a soul anymore, this moment, this fire is proof that he does.

Mila lets out a breath, "Grey."

"Mila," Grey stills for a moment. "You are my world, everything I've ever felt or wanted to feel is right here in your eyes, in your hands."

Mila reaches up unbuttoning his shirt, "And you mine."

Grey is familiar with the Bloodmate ritual through his studies. He wants to explain to Mila but only wants to be with her, feel her from the inside. "The Bloodmate ritual..."

"Shhhh..." Shy says, "just be with me."

Grey complies letting her finish unbuttoning his

shirt as he slides her strap down and off her shoulder letting his finger glide along her buttery soft skin. "You're pure magic." He says licking his lips.

She quirks her brow with a smile cut into her cheek, "I'll show you magic." She unbuckles his belt painfully slow, showing restraint. Mila reaches into his pants taking him into her hands. Grey shudders as she wraps her fingers around his cock, the throbbing intensifies. He blows out a breath and moves her back toward the bed.

He lays her down, "I need more of you."

"Take what you want. I'm yours." She lays back in surrender on the bed.

He spreads her knees apart dragging his lips up her thigh to the warm wet center. With careful strokes his tongue circles the hard nub between her legs. She bucks wildly with pleasure. Heat runs through him and he wants to plunge his cock into her, but also go slow. He slides his fingers inside her as he continues to work her clit with his tongue.

Mila writhes and gasps, calling his name. Her legs are quivering with pleasure as her orgasm builds from her core.

Grey pauses looking up at his beauty. Her lips parted sucking in hard breaths, "Don't you fucking stop." She growls out.

Grey rubs his nose along the warm wet lips of her pleasure, her scent driving him wild. But tasting her, touching her and being with her has nearly restored his control.

He goes down on her again licking her glistening seam, the sweet nectar of her pussy exploding on his tongue. He can't remember ever tasting anything so sweet and satisfying. He buries his tongue deep inside her and slides his hands under her grasping her ass to keep her from bucking away from him.

He lets out a groan the wetter she gets for him. He flicks his tongue on the bundle of nerves that pulses every time he touches her. Her breathing becomes more erratic and uneven, pleasure ribboning through her body. She lets out a long wail of ecstasy and her body stills.

Mila leans up, threading her fingers through Grey's hair. Her eyes on fire with desire, he responds with muffled laugh while nibbling at her folds.

"More." She growls out pulling him up to her.

Grey slowly makes his way to her mouth peppering her skin with hot kisses. He gives proper attention to each breast, sucking her nipple into his mouth, circling with his tongue and giving a nip at the end.

Mila squeals with joy, giggling at the sensation. "That was..."

"The first of many. You are mine, I am yours, and we will spend eternity together in this bliss." Grey lays his head on her chest, his breath leaving a warm trail on her breast, "I've never before looked forward to living forever, until this moment. You've made my existence mean something other than just watching the world change around me. Now, you *are* my world."

"Grey, I've never felt anything like this. Our

kind..." She hesitates, "We have many mates, but I can only ever imagine being with you. I want no other, I only want to belong to each other." Mila says with an air of confusion in her tone. "It's so far out of my nature, but feels so incredibly true."

"We were created for each other, we are Bloodmates." Grey kisses up the soft skin on her neck to her ear. "Meant to be one, together forever." He teases the spot behind her ear with his tongue. The sound of her blood rushing through her veins is pushing him over the edge of control. He struggles to maintain his composure. He wants to sink his fangs into her and drink from her. "For so many centuries, I thought the stories of Bloodmates were nothing but a myth, a fairy tale, but in this moment, knowing that I need to be with you and near you forever, I'm living the fairytale now."

Mila wraps her legs around him coaxing his throbbing cock closer to her. "I need you. Inside me. Now."

"As you wish, my love." Slowly Grey slides his steely length inside her wet walls.

Mila moans at feeling her pussy being stretched open by him, she tries to steady her breathing, "Slow."

"Yes, my love." Grey stills himself, concerned that he's hurting her tiny form. "Are you okay? Am I hurting you?"

"No, I just want to feel every last inch of you as you invade me." Her eyes turn blood red and fangs protrude from her gums.

A breath hitches in Grey's throat as her walls tighten around him. A devilish grin dances on her lips, "Am I hurting you?"

Grey shakes his head no, he eyes her fangs, "Fangs?"

"I'm a blood fairy." She squeezes him again and lifts her hips to take all of him inside her, "I showed you mine, now you show me yours."

Grey stops for a moment, wrestling with his thoughts of keeping his fangs hidden.

"What's wrong?" Concern fills her tone.

Grey's eyes widen as he rhythmically thrusts inside her, "Not a Goddamn thing."

Mila threads her fingers behind his neck and pulls him to her dragging her teeth across his neck, "I want to taste you."

Grey responds with a hard breath, he has a deep need to feed her and satiate her Thirst. He lifts his chin fully exposing his neck to her.

Mila sinks her fangs into his neck and moans as the warm liquid fills her mouth. The sensation running through Grey urges him on. He leans down while she's still feeding on him and gently punctures her neck, the thick blood explodes with an intense flavor and magic that fills his whole body as his Thirst is sated.

Their bodies remain intertwined as they drink from each other creating an unbreakable bond between them. Their bodies move in a smooth and vigorous rhythm.

Nothing else exists in their world, only the sounds of their breath brushing against one another and the soft suckling of each other's blood. Grey feels her pussy tighten again around his shaft. "Mila," he growls.

Mila pulls away from his neck for a moment to look in his eyes. "Yes." She smiles knowingly.

Grey has no words, he looks upon the face of his future. Knowing that as long as he has her, he will be content forever.

Mila runs her finger along the blood on her lip, then moves to Grey's lip, "I love you." She giggles raising her hips to him.

"I love you too." Grey says and continues, "From this moment forward I will feed all of your needs, wants and desires. I will protect you from all that would threaten you. I take you as mine and beg that you will take me as yours for all eternity."

A ragged breath hitches in Mila's throat as Grey speaks while still pumping his hard cock inside her. "I will be yours forever, here for you to feed on; mind, body and soul. I want to be your everything from this day forward and throughout eternity. I want to be yours, and I want you to be mine."

Mila lowers her head then looks up through

hooded eyes, "I submit to you as your Bloodmate."

The crescendo of Grey's orgasm pools in the tip of his dick. He says with choppy breath, "And I submit to you, as your Bloodmate."

Grey can't control himself for one more second, a roar rips through the room dancing on the echo of Mila's cries of passion. "Grey, I'm coming."

"I am too." Grey doesn't stop his rhythmic pumping. He feels her squeeze and spasm around him as he fills her completely.

He collapses sweaty and breathless, careful not to crush her tiny form. "That was..."

"Holy hell," Mila breathes, then playfully licks the blood drying on Grey's neck. "What was that?

Grey's asks, "I thought you knew the Bloodmate ritual."

"Is that what that was?" She asks astounded trailing her fingers along the plane of his chest.

"Yes, we have completed the exchange of blood. Neither of us will ever need to feed from another. Your blood is all I will ever need again." He thinks about it for a moment, "I'm not sure how it works for other races."

Mila smiles and with serious eyes says, "It doesn't matter, your blood is all I'll ever want."

Bliss floods Grey and all of his senses. He can't remember a time when he has ever felt so content. He pulls her tighter into his chest. "This is all I've ever needed in life, and I never knew it."

Mila nuzzles into him releasing a content sigh.

Banging on the door startles them both. "Grey, I know you're in there." Angus' frantic voice comes from the other side.

"Go away, Angus," Grey says pulling Mila closer.

"You've got trouble, Grey and it's heading this way fast," Angus yells through the door. "I'm coming in."

Mila rolls her eyes, "The Brownie?"

"Yeah," Grey says with a laugh.

Angus appears at the foot of the bed, "Oh for fuck's sake." He looks away. "The last thing I wanted to see was your white ass in the air."

"I never said to come in," Grey says pulling the sheets up to cover Mila.

"Vash is coming and he's not alone," Angus says looking away from the couple.

"I can handle Vash," Grey says confidently.

"He's called the 'Home Office'. You're going to have The Directive all over you in short order." Angus' eyes Mila suspiciously. "There was a total of eight bodies at Underground Atlanta."

"What does that have to do with us?" Grey asks.

"Your little blood fairy there likely has some insight on the situation." Angus tips his head toward Mila.

"Are you implying she had something to do with those bodies?" Grey throws his shoulders back in challenge.

"I'll flat out say it! That's why Blood Fairies aren't allowed here, they're cold-blooded killers." Angus says fortifying his stance.

In a flash, Grey is up and has Angus pinned against the wall with his fangs bared, "You watch what you say about my mate."

Angus' features blanch in terror, he struggles against Grey's grip. In a choked voice he says, "Grey, I can't breathe."

"I know." Grey says in a low, threatening voice, "Mila did not kill anyone."

Angus cringes before speaking, "How do you know?"

"She's my mate, I know." Grey doesn't question Mila's innocence for a second.

"But Vash doesn't. He thinks she did it and I'm sure he's told, Clarence. This is an easy win for him. You know how wolves can be." Angus explains.

"I also know how Brownies can be." Grey lowers his eyes to Angus'.

Angus squirms and squeezes his eyes shut. "Can you let me go?"

Grey loosens his grip slightly to allow Angus to speak.

"Whether she did it or not, they're coming for her. I can help you." Angus offers.

"I don't need your help, Angus." Grey quirks his brow.

"But do you want it?" Angus says with a smile cut into his right cheek.

Mila slides out of the bed and stands next to Grey. "How can you help?"

Angus' eyes widen seeing Mila's naked form, he makes a choking sound when Grey squeezes his throat again. "Avert your eyes," Grey growls.

Angus quickly complies turning his head to look out the window, "Wow."

Grey tightens his grip.

"Sorry." Angus chokes out.

"Answer me, how do you think you can help?" Mila asks, truly interested.

"I can create a diversion, buy you guys some time to get out of here." Angus rubs his neck when Grey releases him. "I don't know where you're going to go, it's not like you can hide from The Directive."

"We have no need of hiding from The Directive." Grey takes the sheet off the bed and wraps Mila protectively. "But I have no desire to wait around to negotiate with a bunch of trained dogs."

"They aren't looking to negotiate. They've got

local vamps on the payroll." Angus says as a warning.

"They don't concern me either." Grey pulls his trousers on and looks to Mila, "But we really shouldn't wait around. Negotiating with The Directive will prove more difficult if I've left a carnage of their operatives."

Mila's eyes spark, "You'd do that for me?" She sidles up to Grey nuzzling into his chest.

"I will destroy anyone that so much as looks at you wrong," Grey growls into her ear.

Mila runs a single finger down the center of his well-formed chest, "And I for you."

Grey lifts her lips to his. "My Mila."

Chapter Seventeen

Mila digs in her bag for clean clothes and blows out a frustrated breath. Grey comes up behind her, "What's the matter, my love?"

Mila smiles rolling her eyes, "Nothing to wear."

"Not to worry, I'll get you whatever you need once we're out of here." He assures her.

"Do you really think we can trust him?" Mila ticks her head toward the main room where Angus is.

"To a point." Grey zips his suitcase. "Angus and I have been friends for a long time, he's never betrayed me, but then again, the price has never been right."

"Where are we going to go?" She asks slinging her bag over her shoulder.

Grey takes the bag from her, "Right now, I want to focus on getting out of Atlanta with little to no incident." He takes her into his arms, "Then we find your mother."

A breath hitches in Mila's throat, "My mother?"

Grey nods smiling, leading her by the hand toward the door. "Yes, we're going to find her."

"How did you..." She trails off watching his confident movements, falling deeper for him with every step he takes. "Hera?"

"Yes," he confirms then continues, "Speaking of people we shouldn't trust, she makes the list."

Mila stops in place wanting to defend Hera. "Hera would never betray me."

"I think you are mistaken," Grey says with a solemn lilt in his tone. "We'll talk in the car. But let's get a move on."

Mila knows he's right, Hera was going to take

her back home. She wonders if she ever had any intention of really looking for her mother, or if this was just a patronizing vacation for her.

Angus paces the living room floor when they come in. "What's taking you two so long."

"I had to pack," Grey says coolly.

"You might have moved a little faster." Angus scowls looking out the window. "They're here."

"I know," Grey says moving toward the window. He steps out onto the balcony curling his lip in disgust, "I can smell them."

Banging on the door draws Mila's attention, she looks to Grey, "What are we going to do?"

"Do you trust me?" Grey asks wrapping his arm around her waist.

"Of course I do." She says.

"Then hold on." Grey pulls her tighter in and looks at Angus, "I'll see you next time."

"Hopefully there won't be a next time." Angus shakes his head.

Grey nods and effortlessly leaps over the balcony. Mila holds tight, she trusts him, but jumping from this height is a little daunting for her. She would've preferred phasing out.

They land in front of the valet stand startling William. "Professor Grey."

"William, my keys?" He asks taking a twenty dollar bill from his pocket.

William surrenders the keys with shaky hands. "Thank you, sir, I hope you enjoyed your stay."

"It was delightful as always." Grey unlocks the car with the keyfob, opens the door for Mila and helps her into the car.

Mila watches as he puts the bags in the trunk and joins her in the front seat, his speed is impressive, nothing but a flash of movement and they are already on the road.

Mila watches out the window at the strange world around her. This is the first time she's really felt relaxed, which goes against everything she should be feeling. She's being hunted.

Grey moves the car through traffic with precision, and they are quickly out of the city. She turns several times looking behind them looking for anyone giving chase.

Grey puts his hand on her knee, "It's going to be okay. They'll have a difficult time following us."

"I understand you're more powerful than the werewolves, but Angus said there were vampires too. Aren't you worried about them?"

Grey smiles, "I am not concerned about the other vampires."

"Why? Are you just that good or that cocky?" Mila smiles playfully.

"There are not many other vampires left in the world that are as old as I am, and therefore few that are as powerful as I am." Grey keeps his eyes on the road, his expression softens. "Vampires get better with age."

She squirms in her seat as heat pools between her legs at the thought of being with him again. Her desire for him could never be satisfied for long, she'll always want more of him. She's not sure if it's because he's a vampire or they really are Bloodmates. Her eyes sparkle with desire, "You're going to get better?"

Grey flashes her a glance, “Yes, every moment we’re together it’s going to get better.”

“I could get used to that,” Mila says with a sense of satisfaction.

Mila feels Grey’s whole being stiffen. “What’s wrong?” She asks riddled with concern.

“We’ve got company.” Grey hisses with his eyes darting to the rear view. “How the hell...”

He drops his foot harder on the accelerator.

Mila turns looking through the back window, “I don’t see anyone. The road is all but empty.”

“I can feel them long before I see them,” Grey says gripping the steering wheel.

“That’s a good talent to have.” She says weighing the options. There’s not much, mostly grassy fields and a few houses from time to time. “Where are we?” She asks.

“We’re in Alabama,” Grey says still concentrating on the road.

The engine groans going at top speed, taxing the car to it’s fullest. “What’s in Alabama.”

“Nothing. We’re heading to New Orleans, I have

friends there that can help." Grey says with a tight voice.

"Friends are good," Mila asks still not able to see anyone behind them. "Are we going to make it?"

"Yes," Grey says quickly.

"And once we get there, then what. If these guys are still on our trail what do we do?" Mila asks unsure of what the future holds. She doesn't want to go back to the Underworld, she doesn't want to leave Grey, and she's sure that her father will not be okay with her bringing a vampire back.

"We're going to go to Vivienne's, she's neutral," Grey says.

A flash of jealousy flashes through Mila, "Lover?"

Grey glances at Mila with agrin, "Is that jealousy?"

"No." Mila shakes her head not looking in his direction.

"Vivienne is just a friend." Grey takes one hand

off the steering wheel to caress her cheek, “Mila, there is only one woman for me.”

“Okay.” Mila relaxes, “But if she’s neutral what happens when we get there?”

“I’ll be able to figure some of this out and talk with my friend in The Directive. Explain that you’re innocent.”

“If we can convince them that I am innocent, that doesn’t change what I am and how I’m not allowed to be here,” Mila says with doubt in her tone.

“Don’t underestimate my power,” Grey says with confidence.

“Do you have the power to change laws?” Mila asks pinning him with a look.

“Possibly, or at least make way for an exception to be made,” Grey smirks, thankful for his longtime good standing with The Directive. “I know very little about your race and was unaware of why you can’t be here.”

“Blood fairies are insatiably hungry for human blood. We have a hard time controlling ourselves." Mila shrugs, "And the supernatural beings here value human life."

"You don't?" Grey's tone is curious.

"I value all life." Mila's tone is blanketed in sadness, "But it really isn't a popular opinion among my kind."

"That would explain the ban." Grey nods, "It's going to be okay, no one will take my Bloodmate from me."

Mila believes him, trusts in what he says. "I know."

"Tell me about your world." Grey wants to know more about her.

"It's a beautiful, but dark place. The sun only shines there for a few hours a day, not like here." Wonder fills her voice as she looks out upon the field of flowers.

"Sounds delightful." Grey laughs.

"The sun, how can you be out in the sun?" Mila asks realizing that it shouldn't be possible for him to be out in daylight.

"I told you, vampire's get better with --" Grey is

cut off by a jolt that rattles the car.

Mila spins around seeing a small black car ramming into them. "Grey!" Mila shouts.

"It's okay." Grey attempts to calm her. "I've got this."

"But they're right behind us." She cries out.

"It's okay." Grey focuses on the road ahead. "They won't be able to keep up for long."

Mila shifts her glance between Grey and the car behind them. The vampire behind them cuts a sinister grin into his cheek. She feels him looking through her.

Mila shudders with fear. "He's pure evil."

Grey looks at her with a serious stare, "I can also be pure evil."

Mila is lost in his gaze, the danger all around them melts away in the safety of his presence. She watches Grey as his eyes widen. "No!" Grey yells.

Mila turns in a split second to see the shape of something in the road. Grey jerks the wheel to avoid hitting whatever it was. The car is unable to sustain the quick movement and begins to flip several times. Dirt and debris fly through the air as the car tumbles through the field.

Grey wraps his arms around Mila to get them out of the car, but before Grey can, Mila phases both of them out into a nearby silo. Not a moment too soon, the car bursts into flames in the field. They both watch as black smoke billows from the car.

Relief runs through her as she releases a breath and turns to Grey, "Are you okay?"

Grey scoops her up into his arms and huffs a laugh, "I'm fine, are you okay?" He pulls her to him protectively.

"I am now." She nuzzles into him.

"You're going to have to teach me how to do that." Grey remarks kissing the top of her head.

"Sorry, it's a fairy thing." She pumps her brow.

Mila drinks in the way he looks at her and revels in the heat flowing through her from him.

Movement in the field draws Grey's attention, "We should go."

Mila sees a group of men coming toward them. She doesn't feel afraid, she knows that Grey will protect her.

"Are you ready?" Grey asks.

Mila nods, "How are we --"

Grey lifts her into his arms and takes off at full vampire-speed. Mila digs her fingers into his back holding on.

Some of the men shift into wolves and give chase, but they can't keep up with Grey for long.

She marvels at his speed and how he holds her firm, but gentle as though she's fragile and might break.

She nuzzles deeper into his chest to shield her eyes from the wind. Mila inhales his scent deeply and knows that he is hers.

Chapter Eighteen

Grey dashes through the open fields to the nearest thicket of trees and forest. The cover of the trees will help them gain some ground before they have to go back to more wide open areas.

He laments the loss of his car, this trip would've been much better if he didn't have to run. But he will do whatever it takes to keep his mate safe. Grey can hear the wolves in the distance, but they can't catch up.

Darting through the trees he feels Mila's fingers

grip him, the sensation drives him to maintain his top speed on foot. But being broad daylight, he has to find shelter or a vehicle soon. His strength will wane once the midday sun is beating down on them.

He gazes down at her momentarily her content smile as she's pressed against him fills him with joy. He wants her, now and always.

City sounds can be heard in the distance. Grey has to move fast while he's there. The plan unfolds in his head before they get to Montgomery, Alabama. Grey runs all the possible scenarios through his mind. He needs a fast car, but doesn't want to steal one.

Grey gently places Mila on the sidewalk as they enter the city. "We've got to be careful. Are you okay to walk?"

"I'm fine really." Mila gazes into his eyes missing the full contact she had with him.

"We've got to get a car." Grey wraps his hand around hers.

"Okay, what's your plan for that? I could get us

one." Mila wants to be helpful.

"Really?" He says, "How would you go about it?"

"I can get one." She says reassuring him and motioning to the cars around them, "Just tell me which one you want."

"Just like that?" He asks with a chuckle.

"Yes." She nods.

"I'd rather obtain a car legally." He says lowering his chin.

"What do you mean?" Mila's innocense tickles at his emotions.

"I don't want to steal one." Grey continues down to the sidewalk in deep contemplation of how to get a car fast, "We've broken enough of The Directive laws today, I'd like to not break any others if we can help it. And honestly, none of these cars would do."

"You're going to have to explain some of this to me later." She hurries to keep up with him.

"We can't use magic around non-supers. The Directive is in place to keep supernaturals hidden. It's just better that way for us." Grey truly believes in The Directive's purpose and never thought he'd find himself on the wrong side of their operatives.

"But aren't we on the run because of them?"

"We're on the run because someone is draining humans." Grey points out.

"But I'm not going to be able to stay because of The Directive's rules." Mila hangs her head.

Grey stops and turns to Mila taking both of her hands in his. "Nothing is perfect, and I don't know all the details of why Blood Fairies can't be here. Honestly, The Directive, while stern is also very reasonable."

Mila looks up at him with fear in her eyes. It destroys him to see her so afraid, "I'm going to protect you. If I have to go to Magno Zara and throw myself at his mercy, I'll do it. I know he'll understand and make it right. That's part of what this trip is about."

"How so?"

Grey continues down the sidewalk toward an upscale condo community. "My friend, Vivienne can help us move around undetected for a while and also help me navigate the politics of The Directive as it pertains to Bloodmates."

"So she's part of The Directive?" Concern fills Mila's tone.

"No, but she's very old, very wise and if there's any way we can get out of this mess, she'll know how," Grey assures Mila while looking around to see if anyone's watching. He takes her into his arms to jump over a gate. "She also is rumored to be very friendly with Magno Zara."

"Who's Magno?" Mila says putting her feet back on the ground.

"He's the leader of The Directive." Grey nods.

As he continues through the gated community, he's looking at the garage doors. "Damn it." He says full of frustration.

"What are you looking for?" Mila asks.

"I'm hoping to find one of these garages open," Grey says still scanning the area.

Mila smiles, "Pick one."

He looks down at her with a knowing grin and

points toward the two car garage at the end of the driveway. "That one."

Mila puts her arms around him, pumps her brow, "Hold on."

She phases them into the garage. Grey recovers and looks at the two cars inside the garage. "Yes!" He says balling his fists in victory.

"Find what you were looking for?" Mila asks leaning up against the white Alfa Romeo 4C Coupe. Grey eyes the car and runs his finger along the hood.

"Yes, I did." He nods as he opens the car door. "Now let's hope the keys are in it."

Grey slides down into the car and looks over at the Jeep Grand Cherokee sitting in the other bay. He takes a moment to think and steps out of the car. "I think we should take the Jeep."

"Either works for me." Mila says heading for the Jeep. "But why? The white one looks a lot faster."

"It is faster, but we could need something that can do well in the mud." Grey opens the door for her, and she slides in. He goes around and gets in the driver's side, "But this baby has 475 horsepower, and can travel at a good clip on the highway with decent control."

"People here really take these things seriously?" Mila widens her eyes.

"I take vehicles very seriously," Grey says with a ghost of smile dancing on his lips. He leans across sliding his finger under her chin drawing her lips to his. "I take all things of beauty very seriously." He seers her with a lustful glare.

Mila expels a breath, and her cheeks redden. "I'll remember that."

"I'll remind you." He says pushing the button on the garage door opener. The door lifts open, and he pushes the start button relieved that the key fob is inside the car somewhere.

He pulls the jeep out of the garage, "Can you open up that glove box, please?"

"What's that?" She asks looking around.

Grey points guiding her to the latch, "Right there. There will be some papers with the owner's name and address on it. I want to make sure they are paid for their trouble."

Mila hands him a packet of papers and Grey makes a call on his cell phone. "May I please speak with Carlos?....Yes, I'll hold." Grey finds the remote control for the gate and pulls out onto the street and heads for the highway. "Carlos, I'm fine how are you?....Yes, please have a courier deliver a cashier's check to Andrew Lydon in the amount of one hundred thousand dollars." Grey gives him the address. "Include a note with an apology for any inconvenience."

Grey listens for a moment and asks Carlos to confirm the information, "No, you don't want to know...Thank you." He hangs up the phone.

"What's a cashier's check?" Mila asks.

"It's a check that's as good as cash. It also doesn't have to have my name on it. I want to be sure the owner of the car is paid." He says.

"You're really serious about all this honor stuff." Mila hangs her head, "Things are very different from where I'm from."

"I can't wait to hear all about it and all about

you." Grey says squeezing her thigh. "We've got about a four hour drive if the roads are clear." He lowers his head slightly, "In broad daylight, we need to stay close to the speed limit."

"You don't like to go slow, do you?" She leans over the console of the car whispering in his ear.

"No, I don't." He breathes out. "But I do have to stay focused on the road. No more accidents and we have to watch for operatives. It's unlikely they'll catch up or even be able to find us while we're in this car."

"One thing I do know is that werewolves have an excellent sense of smell." Mila says with concern.

"Yes, but they have to catch up with us first." He ticks his head at the rearview mirror, "I intend to make sure that doesn't happen this time."

"I trust you." Mila says putting her hand on his thigh.

A Vampire's Thirst

Chapter Nineteen

Mila gazes out the window as Grey winds through the streets of New Orleans. "Are we close?"

"We're here," Grey says parking the car on the street.

Mila's eyes convey sadness looking out over a cemetery across the street. She opens the door and jumps out running into the cemetery.

"Mila wait!" Grey calls following after her.

She moves through the cemetery brushing pebbles off the headstones. "Why do you let this continue?" She cries out in anger.

The man standing by the grave says nothing.

"Mila, who are you talking to?" Grey asks looking around.

Mila motions to the man, "He's a Shomer. They don't realise what they're doing."

Grey takes her by the shoulders, "There's no one there."

"There is." She insists, she turns to the Shomer pleading, "Please, you have to let them pass on."

"Mila, what's going on?" Grey asks looking around and seeing nothing but gravestones.

"The Shomers, when they die they continue to guard the graves of those they've watched over after their death. Many of them leave the pebbles on the grave, not allowing their souls to pass on to the next world," Mila hangs her head, "My world."

"I don't understand," Grey says confused. "Your wor --" He stops himself working it out in his mind, "Your world. As in the Underworld, is the actual place you go after death."

"Yes, what did you think I meant?" She says going

to the next grave to brush the pebbles off. "These poor souls are trapped here, unable to move on."

"So to be clear, the pebbles on the headstones keep the dead from moving to the next world?" Grey asks.

"Yes!" Mila pleads, "These Shomers have always had it wrong, they think they are helping by keeping the dead here, but they suffer for eternity in the grave."

"Okay, we take the pebbles off the graves." Grey still doesn't have complete understanding, but he wants to please her. He begins brushing the pebbles off the headstones.

Mila smiles at seeing him helping her, she continues on disregarding the Shomers until she finds herself completely surrounded by them.

"You must stop this." One of the Shomers says in a menacing tone.

"No, these souls need to move on. Not be trapped in their coffins for eternity." Mila says standing her ground. "You're supposed to be guarding them until we take them."

Grey is by her side as soon as she begins to speak, he tries to see who she's speaking to but is unable to see anyone other than Mila.

The Shomers all take a step back from Mila when Grey is by her side. Mila studies Grey trying to figure out why they've all stepped back.

One brave man approaches Mila cautiously eyeing Grey. "Child you aren't supposed to be here." He says in a kind voice.

"Who are you to say where I can and can't be?" Mila demands.

"We are those who decide who goes to the underworld and who stays." He says looking into Grey's eyes then turns to Mila. "You aren't supposed to be here."

"It's not yours to decide who moves on and who stays." Mila pushes past him brushing the pebbles off.

"But you think it's yours?" The Shomer says in a menacing tone.

"It's the natural order." She says. "When they die, they come to us and..." Mila stops at the realization that the Shomers don't know what's next.

"Mila?" Grey says staying close by her side.

"You aren't able to see the men standing right here?" Confusion reigns in Mila's mind.

Grey gazes into her eyes seeing her pain, "I'm so sorry, but I can't."

"It's okay, just keep removing the pebbles." She turns back to the Shomer and tries to explain it to him. "If the dead don't belong with us, we send them where they are meant to go, but no one is meant for this agony, being left in the grave..." Mila waves her hands, trying to staunch her tears for fear of appearing weak.

The Shomer doesn't back down, "Did you ever stop to think some of them chose this?"

Mila looks around at all the graves, many of them still have pebbles on them. "All of them choose this over the afterlife?"

"Maybe they would choose this over purgatory." The shomer says raising his brow. "You don't know."

"And you do?" Mila shakes her head, "No one, not

you, not me get to decide who avoids judgement."

"In the Jewish tradition, they get to decide." He says.

"Mila, you're really worrying me." Grey puts his hands on her shoulders.

"Don't be worried, we're getting the pebbles of the graves." Mila phases in and out until all the pebbles are strewn on the ground. She walks past the Shomer. "It's not your place, or theirs."

The Shomer takes a step back from Grey when he passes by, "But you'll allow him to decide?"

"What's that supposed to mean?" Mila stops in her tracks.

"He's not living, yet he's here." The Shomer says.

"He *is* living." She pins him with a look. "Haven't you seen a vampire before?"

"Mila." Grey says.

"Many, and they don't belong here either." The Shomer's voice sounds like gravel as he grows larger.

Mila doesn't react, she feels a brief sense of panic but knows that Grey will keep her safe. "You don't frighten me. I will do what's right."

"You should be afraid, you have no power here." Another Shomer comes up behind her.

Mila ticks her brow, "You are mistaken." She looks around at the souls leaving the grave heading for the Underworld. "Now they can go home."

Grey is watching on in awe and confusion. He's not able to see anything other than Mila standing up for herself against an invisible force.

Mila nuzzles into Grey, "Okay, we can go now."

He holds her, "I still don't know what happened."

"I've set free the souls of those trapped here. They can move on now." A breath of relief brushes across Grey's chest.

"What in the hell is going on out here?" The voice of an older woman with a thick Cajun accent streaks across the graveyard.

Grey turns around keeping Mila behind him protectively. She remains still behind him, unsure of what threat she's facing now. "Vivienne! Just who I came to see."

Vivienne looks around the cemetery, "Grey?" She

doesn't sound happy to see him. "What have you done?

Mila feels Grey's absence as he steps closer to the woman and embraces her. "I've done nothing. You know me better than that."

"Is that so? The Directive has sent out a notice that you are to be detained on sight, then you show up at my door causing a ruckus in the cemetery?"

Grey turns and looks around, he sees nothing but the gravestones and Mila. "I'm not sure what you mean about a ruckus."

Vivienne brushes past him waving her arms, "Look at them!"

"I don't know what you two are talking about, I don't see anything." Grey squints his eyes trying to see what they see.

Vivienne catches sight of Mila and freezes in place with her mouth hanging open. She goes to her taking her face in her hands gasping, "Genevieve?"

"No, this is Mila." Grey comes to where the women are standing.

Mila fills with hope and dread all at the same time taking a step away from Vivienne, "You know my mother?"

"Your mother?" Vivienne says confused.

"Yes, my mother is Genevieve." Mila says, "Do you know where she is? I have to find her."

Vivienne's expression changes from shock to fear, "You're her daughter...from the Underworld."

Mila nods, "Yes. I am."

Vivienne shakes her head and speers Grey with an angry look. "That explains all of this and shame on you for bringing this to my doorstep." She swats Grey's shoulder as she passes him stomping back to her house. "Come on, let's get inside before you burst into flames or someone sees you." She motions to Mila.

Grey follows behind. "When have you ever cared about The Directive?"

They walk through the red door into Vivienne's shop. The smell of herbs is overpowering to Mila. The lighting is dim and the air filled with the smoke of sage and some other incense. "I don't go out of my way to piss Magno off. I like being on his friendly side."

"Yes, but this is a misunderstanding." Grey tries to explain.

"You have a blood fairy here, what's not to understand?" Vivienne leans down behind the counter. The sound of glass rattling fills the smoky air.

"That's why I'm here, I need you to explain it to me." Grey pleads with her. "And help us stay off the radar until this blows over."

"Way ahead of you." Vivienne puts two small glasses on the counter and fills them with a red liquid, "Drink. Both of you."

"What is it?" Mila hesitates.

"Something to keep you from being tracked, the last thing I need is The Directive in my shop." Vivienne's tone fills with more irritation every moment they're there.

She wraps her arm around Grey's, "We should go."

"No, we're not going." Grey says turning to

Vivienne, "I need your help."

"I don't cover up murders." She says with conviction.

"I would never ask you to," Grey says as though she should know him better.

"You still haven't drank, if you don't, I'll banish you both from my shop." She walks away from them toward a door with a curtain, "Drink."

They both pick up the glasses. Mila watches Grey, she will drink if he wants her to, she trusts him. Grey nods and drinks the potion.

"Okay, I will listen to what you have to say, then you will go?" Vivienne spits out and sits in a brocade chair in the corner of the room. She picks up a deck of tarot cards and starts shuffling them nervously.

"We haven't killed anyone." Grey starts.

"Then who did?" Vivienne gets to the point, "Because..." She motions to Mila and slides one card out of the deck and flips it over revealing the Death card, "It's what *they* do."

"No, I didn't kill anyone." Mila steps forward, "I

came here to find my mother. Some of my father's men came for me."

Vivienne's stare soaks in all of Mila's secrets, "But there's more to it."

"Yes, one of the men is my betrothed." Mila hangs her head. "I think he's responsible for the killing."

Vivienne begins to soften with remorse. "You can't run away from the bonding. If that's what's been laid out for you."

"But I want to decide. I don't want to be with him as his primary. It's why I have to find my mother." Mila stomps across the shop.

"Your mother was a special case, and she's not..." Vivienne trails off as though haunted by the memory of Mila's mother. She shakes herself back to the present. "It's your people's way," Vivienne says as though she's trying to convince Mila that it's the only way. "And it's our people's way to not have your kind here in the human world. You can't control yourselves. Destruction follows you everywhere." Vivienne turns to Grey, "That's why you have to take her back."

"I can't," Grey says pinching the bridge of his nose.

"You *can* and you *will*." Vivienne becomes more stern.

Mila watches Grey trying to regulate his breathing, his fists ball at his sides and through gritted teeth, "No one will touch her, and no one can make her go back."

"Magno Zara can." Vivienne states it as fact.

"Not even Magno can make me give her up," Grey says with confidence that swells in Mila.

"Oh really?"

"Yes," Grey's fangs are protruding from his gums, he's trying to hide them but can't with the threat to his woman, "Mila's my Bloodmate."

Vivienne stills and gasps, "No."

Grey nods, "So she'll be allowed to stay."

"Are you certain?" Vivienne leaves her chair swatting away the herbs hanging from the rafters and goes back to her counter.

"I have never been so certain of anything in my life." Grey wraps his arms around Mila protectively, "I will not allow them to send her back."

Vivienne scrutinizes them through squinted eyes, "Well there's only one way to be sure." She leans down making a terrible racket fumbling through something behind the counter. She places a white bowl on the surface and holds an egg in the air. "Come closer."

Mila and Grey move toward her cautiously, Grey squeezes Mila's hand to reassure her. Vivienne touches the egg to each of their hearts and then cracks it on the counter, emptying the contents into the bowl. Her eyes widen as she sucks in a sharp breath, "I'll be damned."

"Probably." A voice comes from the doorway.

They all spin around to see a very tall, but well-built vampire.

Vivienne smiles knowingly, "Clarence. How are you?"

"I'm quite well now that I've caught up with *them*." He says taking two more steps into the room.

"Clarence," Grey stands protectively in front of Mila.

"I'm rather disappointed that I've had to trek across the country to speak to you." He steps closer to them and stops when Grey's fangs glisten in the light.

"I'm sorry you had to come all this way for nothing." Grey keeps Mila behind him. "You should have called."

"We surpassed a simple phone call in this matter quite some time ago. This escalated far too quickly for that." Clarence pulls his lips to the side, "I'm sorry Grey, she's forbidden. She can't control herself, she's breaking so many laws just by being here." Clarence swats away the hanging herbs as he walks toward them. "This isn't a law cooked up by The Directive, this is part of a treaty among the realms. Those from the Underworld don't belong anywhere but...the Underworld." Clarence is the first one that seems to be trying to rationalize any real reason Mila can't stay. "Her killing spree is a prime example. They're too dangerous."

"I haven't killed anyone." Mila steps out from behind Grey to speak for herself.

"Clarence, it doesn't matter, you can't send her back." Vivienne says coming from behind the counter.

Everyone turns to Vivienne, Mila wonders what's caused her change of heart. "They are Bloodmates."

Clarence wrinkles his brow with concern, "That's not possible."

"It is." Grey smiles wrapping his arms around Mila's shoulders.

"Look." Vivienne comes across the room carrying the bowl and presenting it to Clarence. He looks down at the two blood-red yolks that have merged into one another completely, but still remain two."It doesn't matter, I have to take her to Magno." Clarence says as though he's not convinced.

"No, I won't go." Mila backs away from all of them.

"Clarence, surely Magno will have an interest in a

blood fairy from the Underworld that is Bloodmate to a vampire. The fact that anyone finds their Bloodmate is nearly unheard of as it is." Vivienne argues.

"I've seen a few cases in my time," Clarence says looking down at the eggs. "I would need to see more proof than the ramblings of a crazy old witch."

"Who are you calling old?" Vivienne flashes Mila a secret look to the large bottle of potion on the counter.

Mila understands in that moment that Vivienne wants her to run. Terror and pain run through her at the thought of being separate from Grey. She gazes upon him longingly, but she doesn't want him to be in danger.

Mila doesn't know where to go or even how to hide, nor does she know who to trust aside from Grey.

"Vivienne, Magno will need more proof than this. We also can't break the law, just because she has a Bloodmate. The other factions would nail us to the cross." Clarence huffs a laugh.

"Interesting choice of words, but I think any faction would understand the purest of bonds." Vivienne says pacing, then coming to a stop between Clarence and Mila. With her hands behind her back she waves for Mila to go.

Mila wrestles with the thought of leaving Grey, her insides crumble.

"After all Grey has done, he'll be able to be with her," Clarence says with an edge to his voice. "Providing dead vampires go to the underworld."

When Mila hears Clarence threaten Grey's life, she knows she has no choice but to go. She glances apologetically into Grey's eyes and phases out.

Once outside the shop she phases into the cemetery to the Shomer, "Take me under." She says for lack of a portal.

"I can't, I can only keep you here my dear." The kind older gentleman says.

"I have to find a portal." Mila looks back at the shop and phases away several times. She's drawn to a cemetery on the Mississippi River. She huddles in the corner of a crypt and drinks down the contents of the bottle she took to mask her presence. Tears spill over her lids from the emptiness of being away from Grey. The thought of him being killed because of her is unbearable, she understands that the only way she can save him is to go home.

She considers dying herself and crossing over as the only alternative to being here and so far away from him. But blood fairies are nearly indestructible, closer to immortal than vampires.

Chapter Twenty

"Mila!" Grey calls out as she disappears from the room. He rushes for the door, but Clarence stands in his way.

"I have people outside, she will not get far," Clarence says giving Vivienne the evil eye.

"Don't give me that look, I had no idea what she was going to do. But if you hadn't been acting a damn fool we could've convinced her to go and see Magno. If Magno meets them, I'm sure he will make an exception for her to stay." Vivienne says going back around her counter.

"Now, we've got a frightened blood fairy loose in New Orleans and in a matter of mere moments a crazed vampire." She motions to Grey.

Grey rushes to Clarence grabbing him by the lapels, "Clarence, you'd better pray she's safe and I find her or I won't be the vampire crossing over into the underworld."

Clarence maintains his cool momentarily, "Grey, your friendship with Jana will only take you so far and you've about exhausted your latitude by accosting *me*."

Grey releases him and drags his fingers through his spiky hair. He knows it's no use to go outside, she's long gone. He also doesn't want to lead The Directive operatives straight to her. He has to be smart about this, he has to mislead them, to save her.

Clarence adjusts his shirt, "You will have to answer for what you've done."

"What's that?" Grey says flippantly.

"Aiding and abetting an illegal supernatural." Clarence doesn't wait for Grey's rebuttal, he stalks out the door.

Grey turns to Vivienne in a near crazed state, "I have to find her."

"I know sweetheart. You will." She reaches for another bottle of potion. You have to take this, four ounces every hour and they won't be able to track you. So don't be stupid and leave any other kind of trail." She warns.

Grey nods, positive that he'll be able to find her, but concerned about The Directive finding her first. If Magno gets hold of her, it's over. "Her mother," Grey says as a revelation. "You know her mother."

"I *knew* her mother." Vivienne corrects him.

Grey hesitates before asking, "Is she dead?"

"I don't know, but if she's alive, there's hope." She comes to a stop in front of him.

"How?" Grey asks desperately.

"Her mother is not a blood fairy. If you can prove her lineage, she may be able to stay." Vivienne says.

"If she's not allowed to stay, then I will go with

her. I have to be with her." Grey is determined to figure out a way to be together.

"That's also a problem." Vivienne's voice hitches with warning.

"How?"

"She's betrothed, without the blessing from one of her parents you will not be allowed to be with her." Vivienne tips her chin downward, "So if you do find Genevieve, I suggest you be nice."

"Of course I would be cordial to her mother, but no matter, I'll be able to be with her if her betrothed is dead," Grey says in a low tone.

"It's not that simple. We can get into it more later, but you need to find her. I'll see what I can do about finding out if Genevieve is still alive." She raises the bowl with the eggs to Grey.

"What do you want me to do with that?" Grey asks with concern.

"You already have the bond of the Bloodmates, but if you drink these you will be led right to her." Vivienne's eyes twinkle.

"You are amazing." Grey kisses the top of her

forehead and drinks down the eggs. He feels queasy and unsteady for a moment.

"You'll be fine, give it a moment and go find her." Vivienne urges him. "And be careful, they'll be watching you."

He hears her words feeling the truth in them as he leaves the shop and gets into the jeep. The sun dips lower in the sky. His pocket watch ticks away the moments he's been apart from Mila and now more than ever the inscription has an intense meaning.

He has to bide his time, wait for nightfall to go to her when he will have less of a risk of being seen. The egg has provided a link to Mila, he can feel that she's afraid, but that she's safe for the moment.

"Sit tight my love, I'm coming for you." Grey whispers.

"I know." he hears her voice in his head.

Grey pulls into the driveway of his Garden District home and bolts through the front door nearly crashing into the caretaker, "Penny!"

Penny steadies the wine glass filled halfway with blood, "Professor Hart, are you okay?"

"No." Grey scratches his head momentarily, "How did you know I was coming?"

"A little birdie told me." She motions to a small yellow bird sitting on the inside of the window sill by the door.

Grey studies the bird and makes the connection, "Vivienne?"

"Yes, she had a message for you as well," Penny says offering the glass again.

"I don't need that." He waves it away, "What did she say?"

Penny turns and walks toward the kitchen, "She said I need to remind you to drink."

"I don't need to feed." Grey snaps. "Was that all she said?"

"Her message was quite cryptic." Penny places the tray on the kitchen counter.

"She said something about the origin being last seen in the Lower Ninth Ward."

Grey thinks for a moment, certain that Mila isn't there. "That's all she said?"

"Yes. That was it." Penny says washing and drying her hands. "Can I get you anything?"

Grey slams his fist on the granite counter top. "Damn it, you witches and your vague messages."

Penny startles back a bit, "Don't kill the messenger."

Grey looks down the hallway, rage is taking him over again from the pain of being away from Mila. The little yellow bird sings a sweet song that's raking away at Grey's last nerve.

"Professor Hart." Penny scolds moving down the hallway to let the bird out of the house.

"I'm sorry, I'm just on edge." He starts for the master bedroom. "I'm going to get cleaned up. I'll be leaving tonight."

He takes each step slowly running the words through his mind on repeat. The lower Ninth Ward, why would she want me to go there? There has to be some reason for that.

He catches a whiff of a scent in the air, "Wolves." He rolls his eyes splitting the blinds with his fingers to peer out. Across the street two men are leaning against a lamp post. "As I thought."

He gets dressed and goes back to the kitchen where Penny is cooking something on the stove. "What is that?" Grey asks finding the aroma of human food unappealing. The eggs still wrestling in his stomach remind him of their presence.

"Well, dinner of course." Penny says, "I wanted to be sure we'd have food for your guests."

"Guests?" Grey searches his thoughts. "I'm not having guests."

"Vivienne said you were having your future in-laws over." Penny says in a confused tone, she looks up as though the clarification is in the air, "Or maybe she said something about outlaws." Penny shrugs, "Either way, she said I should prepare dinner."

Grey squeezes his eyes shut in frustration taking a moment to think, was there more to the message?

"Did she tell you what to prepare?"

"Why yes, she said I should make lycan stew. That your mate and her mother would enjoy it when you brought them back." Penny pumps her brow, "I have to say, I'm tickled to meet your new mate."

"Her mother." Grey says it on a breath, "That's it." He takes his jacket and slides it on quickly heading for the back door and stops, "Penny?"

"Yes Professor Hart?" She says with a pleasant shrill.

"What's in lycan stew?" he turns looking at her over his shoulder.

"You leave that to me, dear." She smiles, "Now, be off with you, we both have work to do."

Grey slips out the back door thinking to himself that he should never forget how vicious Penny can be. She's an old witch, with many tricks up her sleeve.

A Vampire's Thirst

Chapter Twenty-One

Mila shivers in the cold, damp crypt she's found safety in. She wants to move around but is terrified of being discovered. Grey is coming for her, of that she's certain. She jumps at every sound outside the crypt, it's worse now that darkness has fallen and the birds have stopped singing.

Comfort covers her at the thought of Grey not questioning her innocence. She worries about being able to prove it, and it doesn't solve the mystery of who's doing the killing. She knows so little of this world, but the killings definitely sound like the doing of a blood fairy.

Mila freezes when she hears the sound of footsteps coming into the crypt. She remains completely still watching the shadow of a figure enter the room.

A flash of red fills her with dread, it's not Grey. It's a blood fairy. Her father's men have found her.

"Mila, my love." Elomere's voice echoes against the stone walls of the crypt.

She sucks in a breath, unable to phase away from him as it will leave a trail that blood fairies can detect. She doesn't want to fight him, since that will mean killing him.

Another scent is on the air catches her attention, it's only faintly familiar.

Elomere calls out to her again, "I know you're in here, I can smell your delicious scent."

Her skin crawls at the thought of him knowing her so intimately. His footsteps draw closer until his legs come into her view as he stops in front of the niche she's folded herself into.

Mila slows her breathing and tries to calm her bloodlust, remaining still as Elomere continues to speak. "Come now my betrothed, I know we've gotten off to a bad start. But it's time we had a new beginning. I want to take you home and we can begin our mating, you will be the mother of my first-born children. You can fulfil your destiny as my primary."

The thought of him touching her, of having his children tugs at her stomach in the worst way. Grey is the only man she ever wants touching her.

"I've already forgiven you for your indiscretion with the vampire. I understand you're young and you wanted to sow your wild oats. But even his friends know that you can't be together. You can't stay here, I've made sure of it now. If you come out and come home with me, I may even spare your vampire lover."

Mila can no longer contain herself at the threat of him hurting Grey. She phases out of the niche and appears in front of him, her eyes glowing white. "I will not be yours."

She draws her power and launches Elomere against the back wall of the crypt.

Elomere recovers with a slight laugh, “Mila, my darling. Please, let’s not quarrel.”

“I’m not going back with you. I’d rather die here than go back to the Underworld alive with you.” She slams him against the wall again.

“You can’t stay.” He grits through his teeth.

“I can, Grey will see to it!” She puffs her chest out, her anger growing by the second.

“Grey can’t erase the bodies The Directive has found, and all of them lead right to you.” He says with an oily grin.

“You killed those people?” Remorse floods her at the thought of all the innocent people that died. “This is why I don’t want to be with you. You have no heart or compassion. You don’t care if I’m happy, you only want the power that comes with being my primary mate.”

“You’re correct, which is why your father knows I’m a suitable mate for his first daughter. He knows I’m the only one that can tame you, bring you back around to our traditions." Mila notices his subtle movement toward her, she knows better than to allow him to get too close.

She raises her hands and pushes him back into the wall. Something unknown stirs in her, an intense power flowing. "I'll never be yours." She vollies the magic toward him. A ball of light travels across the crypt hitting Elomere square in the chest. His body freezes turning to glass.

Mila studies her hands wondering where that came from. How did she do that? She approaches Elomere looking at his pained expression frozen in place. She senses he can still hear her. "Goodbye Elomere."

She starts up the stairs to leave, but there's a familiar, but unpleasing scent is getting stronger. "Wolves." She whispers. She phases out of the crypt, behind the wolves. There are three standing outside, all in wolf form. She phases out again to put more distance between them.

She can feel Grey drawing closer to her and remains quiet hoping he can hear her thoughts.

Warning him of the danger all around her. Wolves, vampires and other blood fairies lurking in the trees. Mila stands in the shadows from the street lights. Two arms wrap around her holding her in place.

She struggles against them, “Hold still, I’m trying to keep you safe.”

“Let me go,” She bucks against him wriggling away. She turns to see the vampire from Vivienne’s shop.

He whispers over his shoulder, “Hera, get her home.”

Hera steps into the light, “Come on Mila, it’s time.”

“Hera?” Mila chokes it out.

“Yes, you’ve created enough problems.” Hera stands next to Mila.

“I can’t leave.” Mila tries to move away from Hera.

“You have to. Your father wants you home.” Hera insists waving her arms. “There’s a portal nearby, let’s go.”

"No, I won't leave Grey." Mila tries not to sound small.

The vampire approaches her with an angry stare, "I'm allowing you to go home as a courtesy to Grey. Otherwise I'd haul you off to The Directive to be held accountable for what you've done."

"I haven't done anything." Mila cries out, "Grey! I'm here!"

Clarence puts his hand over her mouth, "I'm trying to help you."

Mila can't speak, but this doesn't feel like help. She calls out to Grey in her mind hoping he can find her in time.

"I'm going to release you to go home. You will be safe there, you are not safe here. This is your only chance, I suggest you take it." The vampire says with a penetrating gaze. She finds herself only wanting to comply with him.

"I didn't hurt anyone," Mila says quietly walking to Hera's side.

"You murdered several people, I'd say that's enough for me to know you need to go home." he says as his voice softens, "I know it's in your nature and you can't help it. We will see if Grey will be allowed to follow you to the Underworld, but he has to answer for what he's done as well."

"Please don't hurt him." Mila turns in a panic toward the vampire.

"I have a great deal of respect for Grey Hart." The vampire says. "I will do all I can for him, if you agree go home now."

Mila complies as the only way to protect Grey. In her mind she calls out to him again, "I will find you Grey, I will come back for you."

The werewolf from Atlanta runs up to the vampire shifting into human form. "Clarence. She didn't do it."

Hera grabs Mila's arm and drags her through the portal. Mila fights trying to get away, but she can't. Once on the other side Hera closes the portal and drags her out of Cerberus' reach, "I'm sorry. But it was the right thing to do." She walks away.

Mila drops to her knees sobbing. She feels as though her insides are shriveling to nothing. She longs for Grey's touch, his voice, his body to be near her, but fears she will never see him again.

She gazes upon Cerberus standing guard in the center of the circle of portals.

Mila studies each of the portals, she knows her mother found a way to master them, long before she should have been able to. She's going to learn how too if only to get back to Grey.

A Vampire's Thirst

Chapter Twenty-Two

"Mila!" Grey bellows across the street as he sees her disappear into the portal. He uses his vampire speed to reach her, but he's too late. The portal closes, and he feels his sanity slipping away.

"What the fuck Clarence!" Grey approaches Clarence.

"Don't make this worse. I've been very patient and did this for you. She is safe from The Directive now." Clarence says in a stoic tone.

"But what about the one in the crypt?" Vash

says pointing back toward the crypt.

"There's another one?" Clarence's tone is full of irritation.

"Yes, she didn't commit the murders." Vash widens his eyes. "That's what I've been trying to tell you."

Grey paces in front of where the portal was, running his hands through his hair. His anger brews hot and will soon be out of control. He should have come for her sooner, but he thought she was safe. He promised her she'd be safe and now she's gone.

"Is he being held?" Clarence demands.

"He's not going anywhere," Vash says with a smile. "She turned him to...glass."

"Glass?" Clarence asks.

"Yeah," Vash starts toward the crypt.

"Elomere," Grey hisses and dashes to the crypt. Clarence keeps up with him.

"Grey," Clarence says with warning. "Let me handle this."

"He's the reason she's gone," Grey growls.

"No, she's gone because it's forbidden for her to be here." Clarence walks down into the crypt and circles Elomere's glass form. "Curious."

Grey's fists are balled at his sides, his heart is pounding, and his jaw pops with tension. "I want to smash him to bits."

Clarence puts his hand across Grey's chest. "Hold on a moment. This is not the work of a blood fairy."

"I didn't think so, but I saw her do it." Vash says admiring her work, "I wish I had this power."

"Yes, curious indeed." Clarence taps his finger to his chin in contemplation.

Grey is pushing back the madness. He wants to destroy everything in his wake.

"Grey, you need to get hold of yourself." Clarence puts his hand on Grey's back.

Grey's eyes darken with a seriousness that Clarence has seen in him before, "This is as close to controlled as I may ever be again."

Clarence remains silent, he has no words to soothe Grey's pain.

Grey tries to right himself, think straight. What if

she's not a blood fairy? He thinks trying to work it out.

Her mother, I have to find her mother. Grey turns to leave.

"Where are you going?" Clarence stops Grey in his tracks.

"I'm going home." He says with conviction.

"Home?"

"Yes. If I stay here one more moment, I don't give a fuck what you say, I'll smash that son of a bitch to bits." He stops before heading up the steps, "Honestly, I want him to be aware when I destroy him."

"That's not going to happen," Vash says defensively. "We have to get him to the home office, where he will be dealt with."

Grey approaches Vash, rational thoughts and actions slipping away. "If I have to go through a thousand wolves to be the one who kills him, I will."

"Go home, Grey. We will be in touch, be available." Clarence warns him.

Vash snarls at Grey, "I would be careful getting home."

"I don't have to be." Grey starts up the stairs in disgust. He knows there's not much more control left in him and he needs to leave before he tears Vash to pieces.

Grey walks at a normal pace to the car contemplating everything, but mostly obsessing on howto get Mila back, or get to the Underworld.

He drives uncharacteristically slow, hoping that a solution will cross his path. There's a car in the drive in front of his home, his insides tense as he gets out of the car, "Charles."

"Hey there Grey." Charles comes out of the shadows on the front porch. "I hear you're having a hell of a time."

"Get off my porch, Charles," Grey growls and goes into the house slamming the door behind him.

"Did you bring guests?" Penny asks cheerfully.

"Yeah, Charles is on the front porch." Grey stalks up the stairs and into his bedroom.

Charles follows him up the stairs, "So you found

yourself a blood fairy? Bad luck, mate."

"There are a lot of people that will be having bad luck, but I'm not one of them. I will find her." Grey promises. "And I'll bring her back."

"That's a pretty tall claim, there are very few who can open portals to the underworld. Unless you want to go the old fashioned way."

"If I have to, I will," Grey says sitting up.

"That's no way to be thinking." Charles says in a soothing tone, "You're going to get this worked out."

Grey ignores him, he came home because he wants to destroy everything in his path. He feels as though The Directive has tied his hands in all ways and he just wants her back. "Charles, she's my Bloodmate. I'm going to go insane without her. I'm going to do bad things." he admits with a deadly seriousness.

"Bloodmate? That's just a myth." Charles laughs.

"It's not a myth." Grey shakes his head. "I can't think straight without her. I know how I felt once I caught her scent, and I can only imagine what I'm going to do now, knowing that she too is in pain."

Charles takes Grey into his arms like a loving father, "I will help you through this."

"I don't think you can," Grey says falling deeper into anger and despair.

"I'll talk to Clarence to see if there's anything we can do. In the meantime, I'll put some feelers out for someone that can open a portal."

"You would do that?" Grey says astonished at Charles showing any compassion.

"Yes, I made you, you are my progeny, and I love you as such. I'll do what I can. But for tonight. You need to sit tight."

Chapter Twenty-Three

Mila's legs feel heavy as stone with each step that she takes away from the portal. Her gait sluggish, as she approaches the castle. She's filled with dread that she has to face her father and his mates. Dark clouds gather as she walks through the main gates, as they always do. Mila yearns for the warm sun on her face and is wilting without it.

"Mila, I'm so glad you're home. We've been worried sick." Silan rushes to Mila's side. Mila's thankful that she's the first one she's greeted by. Silan has always been kind to her and her favorite of her father's mates.

"I don't want to see my father." Mila says struggling to get up the few steps, "I want to rest."

"Okay, I'll take you to your room, and I'll stall your father, but you're going to have to face him sometime." She warns.

"I know, but I'd like to have the strength to let him know, he has some things to face as well." Mila pins Silan with a serious look.

"I know, we can wrestle that beast after you get some rest. Do you need to feed?" She asks.

The thought of feeding piques the memory of Grey's blood flowing through her. She has no desire to feed, only a desire to taste him again. "No, I'm quite sated." She smiles.

"Are you sure?" Concern flashes in Silan's eyes. "You look very tired."

"I am tired." Mila continues down the dark hallway. The walls shimmer iridescent, Mila always loved the way the stone shines. She searches for the things she loves about home to quell the pain of being so far from Grey. But things she once revelled in, seem pale in comparison to her love for him.

They reach her room, and Silan pushes the door open. “Your father is very pleased that you're home.”

The room is filled with all of Mila's favorite crystal flowers that only grow in the underworld. The room glows in the myriad of color and light from the flowers. “I can see that.”

“You know he loves you very much.” Silan smiles kindly.

“I wish he loved me enough to let me go,” Mila says quietly.

“You know he can't do that.” Silan lowers her head slightly, “You are the first and the daughter of Genevieve. If you are allowed to break tradition then what of the other daughters?”

Mila rolls her eyes, “Yes, what of the other daughters? Wouldn't it be terrible if we all lived happily ever after?”

“What do you mean? Everyone's happy here with our way of life.” Silan challenges her.

"Are *you* truly happy?" Mila searches Silan's eyes for the answer.

"I am." She hesitates.

Mila shakes her head, "Silan, I think you're as close to content as you can be. You've always been a good mate to my father and wonderful friend to me. You're the closest I've had to a mother and appreciate and love you. But I know there is more to life that you want." She takes Silan's hands, "You always told me to strive for what I wanted, but you've never taken your own advice."

"I have what I want." Silan's movements away from Mila contradict her tone.

"Do you? Do you have passionate love that will transcend time and dimension?" Mila's thoughts return to Grey. Somewhere in her heart, she knows that he will find his way to her.

"Nobody has that." Silan says with a smile, "That's something we have in the flash-bang beginning of things."

"I don't have that flash-bang with Elomere. He disgusts me and my father wants me to be

Elomere's primary mate. I don't want that. I don't want to be near him." Mila stands looking out the window at the rolling hills beyond the castle.

"Sometimes being the first daughter means you have to make sacrifices for your people," Silan explains. "You'll find your flash-bang with Elomere or possibly another mate, but this is something you have to do for now."

"Silan, you can't have it both ways. You want me to be happy, but I have to make sacrifices. It's one or the other."

"You can find happiness in the sacrifice. You just have to look for it." Silan explains.

"And what if Elomere is dead?" Mila thinks of how she left him. She doesn't know what happened if what she did killed him.

Silan stops in her tracks, "What do you mean?"

"Exactly what I said, if Elomere is dead we certainly can't be mated." Mila shrugs.

"What have you done?" Silan's cautionary tone darkens the room.

"I-I-don't really know," Mila says worrying her

cuticles. "I felt threatened, and something happened. I don't know what it was, but he..."

"He what?" Silan takes Mila by the shoulders.

"He turned to glass," Mila admits.

"Glass?" Silan whispers releasing Mila to pace the room. "Then what happened?"

"I got away." Mila begins to plead, "He did terrible things up there. He murdered people, drained them dry and tried to blame it on me."

"Oh Mila, this is very bad." She warns.

"How? He was going to hurt me." Mila's voice raises an octave, "I don't see how you're okay with this."

"I'm not okay with this. Your father wouldn't necessarily be okay with this, but no one is going to be okay with you killing a prince." Silan goes to the door and peeks out checking the hallway. "You do not breathe a word of this to *anyone* else. If anyone asks you about Elomere you tell them you don't know where he is. Do you hear me?"

"Yes," Mila says with wide eyes. She sits on the end of the bed and asks quietly, "Would my father really be okay with me mating to someone that would hurt me?"

"Honestly, I don't know, but we've got bigger problems to solve right now, like how to make sure that no one finds out about this." Her voice quivers with fear.

"He may not be dead." Mila points out.

"No, but if it is discovered that you turned him to glass, you may be." Silan kneels down in front of Mila. "Have you ever wondered why your mother didn't stay in the Underworld?"

"Not really, I figured it's because my father is a tyrant and she wanted to live among the truly living." Mila answers.

"It's because it wasn't safe for her here. If it is found out that you possess her power, it won't be safe for you either." Silan takes her hands, "We have to keep you safe."

Mila stops for a moment thinking about what she did to Elomere, "That was my mother's power?"

"Yes, your mother was a crystal fairy. Your father kept that hidden for a very long time. It is still only a whisper of a rumor, what she was." Silan's brow wrinkles with concern.

"Silan, I'm going to ask you a serious question, and I want the truth." Mila awaits her reply.

Silan nods hesitantly.

"Is my mother dead?" Mila raises her brow in challenge.

"I don't know," Silan answers confidently.

"You don't know...that's it?"

"Yes, the last I saw or heard of your mother is that she had gone through a portal to the top. That's it." She rights herself heading for the door. "But what happened to her when she got there is still a mystery."

"So there's a chance I can find her, and a chance I can live up top," Mila says with hope.

"Your mother isn't a blood fairy. Her kind are not forbidden, we are." With that, she opens the door to leave.

A searing pain tears through Mila, her cries of agony fill the room. Silan closes the door rushing back to Mila. "What's wrong? What's happened?"

Silan searches Mila's body for an injury.

"I don't know." Mila eeks out, "Pain, terrible pain."

"I'll fetch the healer and bring some food." Silan gets up to leave.

"No, don't leave me alone." The panic in Mila's voice stills Silan.

"I'm just going to the door. I'll call down the hallway for help." Silan rushes to the door and screams down the hallway.

Mila curls up into a ball trying to staunch the pain, her howls echo through the halls of the castle until the pain drags her under into a deeper darkness.

Chapter Twenty-Four

Clarence vacillates between excitement and dread. The event of a vampire finding his Bloodmate is so rare and beautiful that it is usually celebrated. But whether Magno will be pleased that Grey's Bloodmate is a blood fairy remains to be seen. The implications of keeping a vampire from his Bloodmate are deadly, to say the least. But what of the law? Will Magno make an exception to the treaty and allow a blood fairy to live here?

Clarence laments Grey's lack of discretion. If

perhaps Mila's lineage had been kept a secret there would be a chance.

He picks up his phone and dials, "Jana, how is the most beautiful shifter I know."

"I'm not in the mood Clarence. We've all heard you have a blood fairy problem. I'm packing now." Jana says in a straightforward tone.

"Before you come, there are a few things I think you need to be aware of." Clarence is back to all business.

"I think we know everything. I've spoken to Vash, he's the one that requested I come." She says with the sound of a zipper being zipped in the background.

"Vash isn't aware of everything." Clarence rolls his eyes thinking of Vash's lack of competence.

"Then fill me in, I'm on the way to the airport." She says huffing a breath.

"This blood fairy is Bloodmate to Grey Hart." Clarence lays it out for her.

"Grey Hart?" Jana questions.

"Yes."

"Oh dammit, Grey." She says with disappointment in her tone. "What do we know about the situation, what information can we use to help him?"

"He's a very old, very well-behaved vampire," Clarence says. "He's been solitary for a very long time, one of Charles' creations."

"That may work in his favor, but I'm not sure Magno will be pleased." She's silent for a moment. "We have to illustrate that Grey is an asset to the community. Remind Magno that he's helped The Directive on many occasions and has only had one infraction." Clarence tries to think of any angle that will help.

"Really? What, did we bust him for jaywalking?" She laughs.

"No, he went on a rampage during World War Two," Clarence remembers the time all too well.

"Battlefield?"

"Yes and villages." Clarence doesn't want to revisit this incident but wants to convey to Jana and Magno that Grey is not a bad vampire.

"I remember that." Jana says, "That's when I first

met him. We let him off though."

"Yes, the circumstances were...drastic." Clarence hesitates. "A young man, whom Grey had taken under his wing was killed in battle. They were very close, Rupert was his name." Clarence remembers. "Had just become a father."

"Yes, I remember how distraught Grey was, he lost his mind," Jana recalls.

"To this day, he still gives to a trust fund that Rupert's grandchildren benefit from. Never will any person descended from that man want for anything."

"Sometimes, Grey is too soft-hearted." Jana smiles, "I just wonder if this is one of those cases."

"It's not, this is different." Clarence argues, "We have to consider that she's his Bloodmate and the fact that there haven't been any issues since the war. He's a good guy and he needs our help."

"That's not what we do," Jana says quickly.

"We keep the peace and the secrets. If we want to continue to do that, Grey needs our help."

"Contain him, I'll be there as soon as I can," Jana

says wanting to get off the phone.

"That could prove problematic."

"How so? You're a strong ancient vampire..."

"Yes, but so is he. I've never had to go head to head with him, but I'm not sure if I can handle him alone." Clarence hates to admit that. "That's why there have been some things he's helped The Directive with, we needed his power."

"We'll do what we can. I'll speak with Magno before my flight. Perhaps he can provide some direction." Jana unceremoniously hangs up.

Clarence studies the phone for a moment. He ponders the thought of a vampire as ancient as Grey finally finding a Bloodmate. All of his centuries spent alone and to finally find true love to have rules stand in the way of him being with her. Clarence would never admit it that he has a soft side, but wants to be careful in how he wields it. He has to maintain control of this situation, but also help Grey.

He pauses in front of Grey's home. How he's going to make all of this work is beyond him, but he doesn't believe they will be able to manipulate an entire treaty based on the love of one vampire. But he has hope.

Clarence walks up the steps to the home and rings the bell. Penny answers the door, "Well hello Mr. Collins, we weren't expecting you."

"You should have." Clarence looks past her into the house.

"Professor Hart is not receiving guests at this time." Penny stiffens momentarily. "But I'll be happy to deliver a message."

"I need to see him now," Clarence tries to take a step through the door, but is halted by some sort of forcefield.

Penny smiles. "That won't be possible."

Clarence huffs a laugh, "I'm here to help him. I can get inside the house, your barrier won't keep me out for long."

"My barrier will hold up nicely, thank you." Penny lays on the thick southern accent.

"Penny, let him in," Charles calls from the parlor.

"Mr. Collins, it would seem Mr. Borne will be

receiving you in the parlor." Penny stands aside and removes the magic barrier from the doorway.

Clarence does nothing to hide his aggravation as he enters the parlor. "I know every vampire likes to have a revenant, but did you have to pick Jenny Greenteeth?"

Grey leans up on the couch covered in sweat with dark circles under his eyes, "Penny is not my revenant, she's my housekeeper."

"Holy hell, Grey you look like...." Clarence can't meter his shock at Grey's appearance.

"Death?" Grey finishes for him and wipes the sweat from his brow. "It wasn't this bad the first time I died."

"What happened?" Clarence takes a seat and acknowledges Charles.

"Mila, you sent her back to the underworld," Grey says with a forced smile . "I do believe that this is akin to my Bloodmate dying and therefore I will be soon to follow."

"We're working on it, Grey." Clarence makes the realization that they'd better work faster.

Grey reaching into his pocket and taking out his watch, he flips it open and studies it for a moment before putting it away, "We're running out of time."

Clarence huffs a laugh, "For a man who's lived many centuries, I find it very pedestrian of you to always be so concerned about time. Patience, Grey."

"For centuries, time is all I've had." Grey starts, his expression pinches with pain. He glances down at the watch again. "But time has a way of showing us what really matters."

Clarence and Charles both still in silent contemplation. Charles shifts uncomfortably in his seat before getting up, "What matters is getting you better."

"What matters is being with Mila." Grey snaps the pocket watch closed. "We're running out of time."

"Jana's on her way, and we're going to speak with Magno, to see if he can make an exception to the treaty." Clarence offers Grey hope.

"I'm not sure what I'm going to do if an exception

can't be made, other than join her in the underworld." Grey shrugs having grown used to the idea, he huffs out, "The problem is, even if an exception is made, her father may not let her come back. He has full dominion over her."

Clarence considers what Grey's saying and exchanges a knowing look with Charles. It is very well-known that vampires are not allowed among the blood fairies in the underworld, they hold a grudge against vampires for Magno not allowing them to feed here. Grey will be a ghost with no home. "We're not going to let that happen."

"Thank you." Grey remains as stoic as possible.

Penny enters the room with a tray of wine glasses filled with blood, "Gentlemen, refreshments?"

Clarence takes a glass, "Thank you."

Charles also takes a glass and drinks it down instead of sipping it politely.

Grey declines the offer, "No thank you."

"I tell you, it's those eggs making you sick." Penny's mouth twists with concern.

"Eggs?" Clarence asks.

"Yes, I drank the eggs from Vivienne to find Mila," Grey says.

"You have an unhealthy trust of witches, old friend," Clarence says eyeing Penny.

Penny leaves the room glaring over her shoulder at Clarence.

Charles sits with the men crossing one leg over the other. "We have an angle."

Clarence inhales a breath, Charles always has an angle, it's rarely feasible and never legal, "What is it?"

"Mila's mother," Grey says.

"How can that help?" Clarence squints his eyes.

"It is believed that she is here, and has been living among us for at least a century without any incident at all. I don't think there's a vampire alive that can say they've never had an incident." Charles offers.

Clarence studies a silent exchange between Grey and Charles. He interrupts their thoughts, "So if we are able to find the mother, there's a risk that she could also be sent back. We can't have them running all over the place. It's bad enough we've got one made of glass in New Orleans."

"That's the other thing," Grey perks up briefly, "We need to kill him."

"Grey, let's not get too hasty," Clarence warns. "We don't even know who he is."

"I do. He's Mila's betrothed. He's cruel to her, and she does not want to be mated with him. Even if I die and can't be with her. I don't want her to have to spend an eternity with him."

Penny stands in the doorway, "I don't mean to be the harbinger of doom, however, doesn't it stand to reason that if you are experiencing this illness due to separation from your Bloodmate, she would be weakened?"

"I hadn't thought of that." Grey gasps. "I have to get to her." He tries to stand from the couch.

"No, you need to stay put." Charles holds his hand up to him.

"The difference is, she won't die. She'll be stuck in the cycle of illness forever." Grey breathes it out and dies inside at the thought of Mila being in pain.

"But if I die and go to the Underworld...even if we aren't allowed to be together, my proximity to her will spare her this pain."

"It's not going to come to that," Clarence reassures him. He isn't sure himself if that's how it will be, but he's not willing to give up just yet. "Let's focus on finding her mother, what do we know?"

"Her mother's name is Genevieve. Vivienne knows her, but says she hasn't seen her for a very long time. That she's not even sure if she's still alive."

Clarence picks up his phone. "Let's see if anyone knows anything. Although, I'm assuming everyone will be very tight-lipped about a blood fairy living among us."

"I don't think that's a good idea, Clarence," Charles warns.

"Why?"

"If we put Directive feelers out for her, it could make her burrow deeper to stay hidden." Charles reasons.

"You're right, she'll become even harder to find," Clarence places his glass on the table.

Penny quickly comes in to retrieve it. "Another?"

"No, thank you," Clarence says without looking in her direction. "We'll find her."

Grey groans at a sharp pain ripping through him. "Fast, we need to do it fast."

"We will." Clarence turns to Charles, "I think we're going to need your particular expertise. I know you have all the seediest connections in every city. We should start there."

"I'll get on it." Charles gets up and leaves the room.

Clarence watches Grey writhing in pain. "Grey, I'm going to speak with Magno. He has to know what's happening to you."

"Thank you."

Clarence pushes himself out of the chair. "I am concerned about your fragile state, I fear your vulnerability may not be survivable in the best of circumstances."

In a flash Grey has Clarence up against the wall,

snarling, “Don’t mistake my pain for weakness. My docile nature prevails in most situations, but in matters having to do with Mila I am far more deadly than I have ever been. You might bring that up when you speak with Magno Zara.”

Clarence smiles, “Just testing the waters, friend. I need to know what type of fight we may have on our hands.”

The ambiguity of who the fight is with is not lost on Grey. “The fight of your life.”

Clarence smiles, “Then let us hope we are all the victors.”

Grey releases him and stalks back to the couch. He pulls his watch out again studying it.

A knowing smile lights Clarence’s features. “That watch.”

Grey flashes a glance at Clarence through his darkened eyes. “Yes.”

“You’ve never forgotten have you?” Clarence asks in a quiet tone.

“How could I forget?” Grey asks as though it’s obvious.

"Rupert was a good man, and he'd be long dead by now regardless of what you did." Clarence attempts to bandage an old emotional wound.

"But he deserved to have more life, more time." Grey argues.

"It's not for us to decide, war is a messy business. Rupert knew that." Clarence says nodding his head.

"But he never had enough time to figure out what really mattered," Grey says choking back his emotion.

"No, but he knew you would. That's why he gave you that watch before he died and now you've had enough time to figure out what really matters. Don't lose sight of that. We're going to figure this out."

Chapter Twenty-Five

Mila opens her eyes to Silan sitting on the bed with her holding a warm cloth to her head. She opens her mouth to speak, but her voice is hoarse and won't come.

"Shhh." Silan tries to comfort her dabbing Mila's cracked lips.

"What's happening?" Mila squeaks out.

"We aren't sure. The healer said she'd be back shortly when she has some answers." Silan smiles.

"I need Grey." Mila whispers, "That's all I need."

"Don't be silly. You're a blood fairy."

"Grey is my Bloodmate," Mila explains, "We need each other. Being away from him is worse than death. You have to get me back top side. It's the only thing that will help."

"I'm sorry, but that's not going to happen." Silan fluffs Mila's pillows, "Lay back, get some rest. The healer will be back soon."

"Knock knock." A sweet sounding voice comes from the doorway.

Mila and Silan exchange a sour glance. "Come in, Sazi," Silan says with a labored breath.

A young woman with flowing blond hair, piercing green eyes and pregnant belly come waddling through the door. "Mila! I'm so glad you're home." She stands next to the bed and slowly lowers herself down. "I'm sorry you're not feeling well. Your father said you just need to feed and you'll feel better. I've brought a little something for you if you're up for it." She claps her hands together and a shirtless man walks through the door.

His chiseled chest and washboard abs would have interested Mila before, but not now. She only has a thirst for Grey.

Mila rolls over and away from Sazi. "I'm not hungry."

"But he's delicious!" Sazi squeals, "I had some this morning. I *am* eating for two."

The man comes around to the side of the bed Mila's facing. "Hey there Mila. I'm here if you need me."

"Ty," Mila recognizes him as a regular feeding partner.

"I'd like to help if I can." He leans down close to her.

Mila's stomach turns at the thought of feeding from him, "I'm really not hungry, but thank you."

"You need to eat something, or you're going to waste away." Krovo's gruff voice fills the room before he does.

"I'm not hungry, Daddy." Mila doesn't turn over or acknowledge him.

He dismisses Ty, “Thanks for trying, we’ll try again later.”

“Of course. Just call, I’m always here for her.” Ty tenderly strokes Mila’s cheek.

Mila cries out in pain as the flesh beneath his touch withers.

Krovo snatches Ty’s wrist, “What have you done?”

Ty stumbles backward, “Nothing, I’ve just touched her cheek.” He studies his hand.

“Look at her.” Krovo points to her cheek. He reaches down to touch her, and she shies away. “Mila, let me touch you.”

“It hurts.” She whines but complies with her father.

He runs his finger along her cheek, and nothing happens. He turns back toward Ty, “You had to do something.”

“I would never hurt Mila.” He says defensively.

“Krovo, calm down.” Silan stands up resting her hand on Krovo’s arm. “Ty would never hurt her.”

“Get out of here.” Krovo shoos him out the door.

Ty complies quickly leaving, but stops to look

back at Mila filled with concern, "Feel better, and please call upon me if you need me."

Mila doesn't answer, she's far too deep in her pain at this point. She mumbles something, but then lays back staring at the ceiling praying for the pain to stop.

"You're going to be okay," Silan says stroking her cheek. "We're going to figure this out."

"Where's that damn healer?" Krovo bellows.

"I'm right here, get out of the way." An older woman enters the room carrying a plate of herbs.

"Keelie, have you figured anything out?" Silan asks with concern.

"I believe I have. We have a solution, but you're not going to like it." Keelie addresses Krovo directly.

"Will it save her?" He asks.

"Possibly." She waves everyone away from Mila's bedside. "Mila, sweetheart, I'm back. I have something for the pain." She lifts a small vial of liquid to Mila's chapped lips. "Drink now, it will help."

"What is that?" Silan's tone is full of concern.

Keelie turns to her, "Let's see it works first."

Mila straightens slightly in the bed, coming back around. She's still very weak but able to speak. "That tasted awful."

"Medicine isn't supposed to taste good." Keelie answers. "Are you feeling better?"

"Not by much, but the pain comes in waves. I feel like I'm withering away." Mila lifts her hand that is visibly wrinkled as though she had aged twenty human years.

"This should help, we're working on other solutions as well," Keelie assures her with a nod. "You have to tell me about this vampire and where we can find him."

"Grey." Mila's spirits lifts slightly saying his name.

"Yes, Grey." Keelie says drawing a long breath. "I believe what's happening is you're going through withdrawal from his blood. That there was an addictive factor to it. So we need to get some of his blood to wean you off slowly so as not to shock your system."

"It's not his blood that's addictive. It's him. He's my Bloodmate." Mila struggles past the lump in her throat. "I need to be with him."

Keelie straightens up, her expression twists to deep concern.

"Keelie? I don't like that look?" Krovo says cautiously, "What is a Bloodmate?"

Keelie says with a smug look on her face, "Krovo, you'd better be ready to welcome a vampire to court. She has to be with him, or they will both die."

"There has to be another way. There's no way I'm allowing her to be with a filthy vampire." Krovo paces the room, "You hear me Mila? No vampires."

Mila looks upon her father with sadness that he would allow his prejudice to kill her.

"Besides, we're immortal. We can't die, this is bullshit, Keelie, I can see right through what you're doing." Krovo barks at her, but she doesn't back down.

"I'm not doing anything, and you're correct. She won't die. But she will wither away to nothingness, she will be in a state of pain for eternity." Keelie says pulling her lips into a tight line.

"His blood can keep this from happening?" He asks working something out in his head.

"It will sustain her for a time. But for her to be truly happy, she has to be with him," Keelie sits beside Mila on the bed.

Sazi stands up, "Mila, you don't really want to be with a vampire, do you?"

Mila nods and whispers, "I want to be with Grey."

"You can't, that's all there is to it. You are my first daughter. It's your duty to mate with Elomere and have lots of his babies." Krovo stubbornly paces the room.

"You can't have babies with a vampire," Sazi says.

Silan rolls her eyes and looks at Mila, "Perhaps

having children isn't the only thing that will fulfill her in life."

"Was that a cut on me because I can still bear children for our mate?" Sazi puts her hand on her hip.

"No, I was simply stating that we all may not want to follow the same path." Silan says with restraint.

"That's not entirely true." Keelie interjects hoping to stop the women from fighting.

"What's not true?" Silan asks.

"A vampire can have offspring with their true Bloodmate." Keelie nods.

Mila's eyes light up at the thought of being able to bear his children. The color returns to her face momentarily.

Silan leans down to Mila and whispers in her ear, "Tell me where to find him."

Mila whispers back to her, "New Orleans."

Silan stands from the bedside. "I'm going to find him and bring him back."

"The hell you are." Krovo protests, "I forbid you

from going there. Do you know what can happen to you if you're caught?"

"Do you realize what will happen to your daughter if we do nothing?" Silan challenges Krovo.

"I believe I have another solution. It may not work, when I created it I wasn't aware that I was dealing with a Bloodmate." Keelie looks upon Mila with worry.

"We have to do something." Silan shifts her eyes to Mila, she can see her wasting away.

Keelie leans down toward Mila. "I'm going to give you more of this potion."

Mila nods slightly and tips her chin up to take the potion. She swallows it down. "What is it?"

"It's forget me potion. It's possible that will cure you." Keelie says putting the stopper back on the bottle.

Mila's eyes fill with terror, "I don't want to forget him, I want to be with him."

"Good job Keelie, perfect." Krovo pats Keelie on the back.

"If this doesn't work you may have to get used to the idea of having lots of little vampires running under foot, Grandpa." Keelie pokes Krovo in the stomach on her way out the door.

Krovo approaches Mila's bedside, "You understand this is all for your own good."

Mila spears him with an angry look but does not speak. In her periphery she sees Silan slipping out the door. Silan winks at her before quietly clicking the door closed.

Mila shifts back to her father and Sazi by the bedside. "You're going to get better and all this will be behind us. You'll be mated to Elomere by the next moon."

A satisfied smile stretches across Mila's face at the thought of Elomere being dead.

"See Sazi, she's already getting used to the idea." Krovo puffs his chest out proudly.

Mila's grin becomes more menacing by the second. Sazi notices before Krovo does, "Mila, what's going on in that mind yours?"

Mila smiles and whispers out on a hoarse voice, "Elomere is dead."

Chapter Twenty-Six

Grey struggles to hide his pain. His insides are turning to ash, but his need to reunite with Mila pushes him forward. He managed to slip out of the house under the watchful eye of Charles and Penny. Easy stuff for him. They likely think he's still resting in the parlor, he laughs out loud as he brings the car to a stop on Florida avenue in the Lower Ninth Ward.

Grey recalls the message sent by Vivienne. He'd like to call her but doesn't want The Directive to know he may be close to finding Genevieve.

"If I were fairy, where would I be?" he says out loud trying to work out her location.

He's hoping there's some sort of cosmic draw to her from his connection with Mila, but there's nothing.

A young woman walks past his car, he can hear her blood pumping through her veins. He doesn't feel as though he needs to feed, but the Thirst is coming back, and he's losing himself to it. He gets out of the car and follows behind her.

Far enough away to not be noticed, but close enough to smell her blood. He stalks closer.

Grey doesn't have the strength to fight the Thirst, he's going to drink from her, and he's going to enjoy it.

Grey is within arms reach of the woman, he's ready to strike, his fangs protruding from his mouth.

He stops in place when he feels a cold blade up against his throat and the serious voice of a woman. "That would not be wise, vampire."

Grey attempts to collect himself, relieved that

someone stopped him, but still crazed from the Thirst. He's fighting it, but losing. He starts to turn around.

"I didn't say to turn around, you wouldn't want to lose your head." She says.

"Thank you," Grey says quietly.

"For what, spoiling your dinner?"

"For keeping me from doing something I'll regret." He says. "May I turn around?"

"Slowly. But know I will not hesitate to end you." She keeps the sword at his throat.

Grey turns around, he can't believe his own eyes. He must be going mad, "Mila?"

The woman freezes in shock for a split second then hardens her stance, "How do you know that name?"

"She's my..." Grief descends on him crashing down all over again. "Bloodmate."

"Who are you?" She demands.

"I'm Grey Hart, and I'm looking for Mila's mother, Genevieve." He gets the sentence out past his dry throat.

"Nobody's called me by that name for a very long time." Genevieve relaxes slightly. "Why are you looking for me? Are you with The Directive?"

"No, I'm looking for you because Mila needs you." Grey pleads with her. "She's been taken back to the underworld against her will, and I need to find someone that can open a portal so I can get her back."

"And you think I can open a portal to the Underworld?" She laughs, "Yeah, I'm not opening anything to the Underworld." Genevieve sheathes her sword. "Get out of here, and if I catch you here again, I will kill you."

"But Mila needs you." Grey's confusion rides out on his tone.

"I can't help her." Genevieve walks away from Grey.

"You have to. You can't leave her there." Grey follows after her.

"I have left her there for a very long time. She can't come here, or I would have brought her back with me." Genevieve wears a mask of sorrow that deepens at the thought of Mila being without her.

"You came here. Why can't she?" Grey rationalizes.

"Because she's a blood fairy, it's forbidden. It's why this is the only place I'm somewhat safe." She rolls her eyes, "Except for the vampires, it's pretty calm."

Grey thinks for a moment, there's an idea brewing that might save his love. "But she's not full blood fairy."

"So? Do you think The Directive is going to care? It doesn't make her any less blodthirsty." Anger flashes in Genevieve's expression.

"Yes, because she's my Bloodmate. It's very rare but very serious. The Directive may make an exception for us, especially since she's not full blood fairy." Grey is talking out loud, but working the idea up as he speaks. "You have to come with me. Clarence will want to speak with you."

Genevieve huffs a sarcastic laugh, "Clarence Collins?"

Grey nods, "Yes."

"He thinks I'm dead and I'd like to keep it that way. It's safer for me to be dead." She says walking in the other direction.

"I will protect you." Grey offers.

"I don't think you can protect me from Clarence Collins." She raises her brow. "You didn't even hear me coming."

"I have the Thirst because Mila's been taken away from me. But I can assure you, I am stronger, faster and far more deadly than Clarence Collins."

"I'm going to have to pass." Genevieve erects a crystal globe around herself and begins to disappear.

"Mila is going to die a slow and painful death," Grey calls out.

The ball stops glowing, and Genevieve comes back. "What?"

"The Thirst, if we are apart the Thirst will consume us both," Grey says, "Look at what it's doing to me."

"Yeah, you do look like shit. When was the last time you fed?" She asks.

"Yesterday." He raises his brow. "Can you imagine what it's doing to her?"

Genevieve looks up to the sky contemplating her next move. She pulls her lips to the side and pins Grey with a hard look. "I'll open the portal."

"Excellent, thank you." Grey releases a breath. "We just have to convince Clarence to let her stay." Grey starts toward his car. "Come on, let's go."

"I said I'd open the portal, I didn't say I'd meet with The Directive." She stands her ground.

Grey considers Genevieve's half-hearted offer. He's never had a child, but can't imagine ever letting them go the way Genevieve has. "How can you be so heartless?"

"It's called survival." She bites. "Do you want me to open the portal or not?"

"I do, We have to go to her." Grey knows that's the most important thing.

"First, that would be *you* going to her. I'm not going." She starts to walk away.

"Holy hell woman, do you care about your own daughter?" Grey yells walking after her.

Genevieve stops, "Listen, vamp, you don't know what you're getting yourself into. Once I open the portal, and you go through, you're going to have to deal with Cerberus, then if you make it through that you'll have to deal with Krovo. He's never going to let you take her."

"You can get me past Cerberus." Grey's eyes lighten, "Then we can deal with Krovo." Grey thinks for a moment not knowing who that is. "Who's Krovo?"

"Her father." She continues walking, "I'm not up for a reunion with the ex if it's all the same to you."

Grey is driven forward by the thought of being near Mila again. He'll face any trial to get to her. "Fine, open the portal, I'll deal with the rest."

"That's where we're going." She snaps at him.

"You can't do it here?" He asks.

"No, you have to be at a weak point in the veil. There's one not too far from here." Genevieve doesn't turn around. "And unless you're a blood fairy, you need one of these." She holds up a small black globe that shimmers in the absence of light.

"What is that?" Grey asks.

"It's a portal key. They are always there, just not always open." She says continuing forward.

Grey stays a few paces behind her. He takes out his phone to send a text to Charles.

Found Genevieve, she's opening a portal. I'm going to get Mila. ~Grey

He flips the switch to silent on his phone before Charles' text comes through.

Where are you? I'm coming. ~Charles

Lower Ninth Ward. ~Grey

They walk into the cemetery where Grey found Mila earlier. They go to the spot where Hera took Mila through the portal.

"Stand back, this will take a moment. And be at the ready, you never know what might be waiting to come through on the other side." Genevieve waves her arms in a circular motion with the globe in her hand. A portal appears in front of them.

Genevieve takes several quick steps backward and draws her sword.

"Thank you," Grey says taking a step toward the portal.

Genevieve puts her arm out stopping Grey, "I didn't open it. There's someone or something coming through from the other side."

The form of a dainty woman with wild red hair blowing in the vortex emerges from the portal. Genevieve lowers her sword slightly with her mouth agape.

The woman from the portal sucks in a sharp breath, "Genevieve."

The air is rife with tension as Genevieve's stance waivers, "Silan."

Grey leans down slightly, "You know her?"

"Yes, she's Krovo's second." Genevieve doesn't take her eyes off of Silan.

Silan moves toward Genevieve with arms outstretched. "Thank the heavens you're alive."

Genevieve drops her sword and her guard. She throws her arms around Silan. "Of course I'm alive."

They try in vain to hold back their tears of joy at seeing one another. Genevieve releases Silan and studies her from head to toe, "Why are you here? Do you understand how dangerous it is for you?"

"It's Mila. She's dying. I've come to find the vampire called Grey." Silan's eyes lower to the ground.

Genevieve looks up at Grey and says with astonishment, "You were telling the truth."

"Yes, I was, and I have to get to Mila, now." Grey starts for the portal.

"Are you Grey?" Silan asks.

"Yes." He doesn't stop, he continues toward the portal.

"Wait," Silan calls out. "There are some things you need to know before you go."

"All I need to know is that Mila needs me," Grey says almost to the portal.

Silan holds her hand up and makes a closing motion, in an instance the portal disappears.

Grey's whole being fills with anger. He turns around stalking toward the two women, "I need to get to her."

Genevieve opens her hands conjuring a spell that she shoots directly at Grey's feet. He's momentarily frozen. "I need to get through that portal." He breaks free from the crystals that were holding him.

Surprise twists Genevieve's features, "How old are you?"

"Old enough that I stopped counting long ago." He answers.

"I'll get you back there. I want to save her, but if you go running through, half cocked you're going to get yourself killed. If you die, there will be no hope for her." Silan argues with Grey.

"Please, we need to get to her." Grey's losing his mind, his strength is still present, but his control is waning.

"We'll go, but first you have to follow my lead, do not speak out of turn." Silan scolds.

"Why can't I just go and get her, bring her back?" Grey asks turning toward where the portal was.

"Because you do not have clearance to bring her back yet." Clarence's voice comes out of the darkness before he does.

"Shit." Genevieve hisses as Clarence approaches her.

"Genevieve, I thought for sure you would stay dead this time," Clarence says walking past her.

"Yeah, well, you can't keep a good girl down." Genevieve offers him a sardonic smile.

"Please, can we open the portal." Grey pleads. "I don't care if I can come back, I have to get to her."

Clarence approaches Grey, "You need to calm down. We're going to get you to her, but we can't bring her back just yet. Not without Magno's approval."

"She's not a blood fairy." Grey protests.

"Grey you're not making sense. You're losing it man," Clarence warns.

"I can't think clearly because being without her is driving me insane. I'm using all my self control to keep from ripping your fucking head off right now." He turns to Silan and in a deep monstrous voice demands, "Now open the Goddamn portal."

Silan jolts with fear and looks to Genevieve for guidance. Genevieve nods urging Silan to open the portal.

"Grey," Clarence calls out. "What do you mean she's not a blood fairy?"

"Genevieve is her mother, she's only half blood

fairy." Grey is only focused on staying directly behind Silan who's walking toward the portal. He doesn't see the wolves closing in on the group.

"I'm not sure that will make a difference. We'll be waiting for you when you come back." Clarence warns.

"I'm sure." Grey nods and turns back toward the portal to walk through.

Genevieve watches as Grey goes through, then exchanges a glance with Clarence. She says nothing as she takes metered steps toward the portal and disappears inside.

Chapter Twenty-Seven

The trio come out the other end of the portal into the Underworld. Grey marvels at the deep purple sky that resembles a stunning twilight back home. A huge three headed dog sleeps deeply in the center circle surrounded by stone structures that appear to be permanent portals. A breeze ruffles Grey's hair when Cerberus exhales.

One of the heads opens one eye lifting up. Silan raises both of her hands, "Oh great Cerberus, let us pass."

Cerberus comes closer to Silan and inhales deeply taking in her scent.

Genevieve tugs at Grey's jacket, "Let's go. I've seen this get ugly."

"We're just going to leave her?" Grey asks in horror.

"She'll be fine, it's us that have to worry." Genevieve continues walking quickly until they are out of site from the circle of portals. "Blood fairies are allowed to pass, Cerberus will let them through along with a few other races. Otherwise, you have to be dead to get by, but good luck getting out once you're in."

"It's a good thing I'm immortal." Grey watches for Silan to join them.

"Immortal is different from indestructible." Genevieve quips.

Grey considers her words as a threat. He doesn't know how to read Genevieve and doesn't quite care. He's getting to his one true love, his Bloodmate and not a giant three headed dog or crazy fairy with a sword is going to stop him.

Silan comes down the trail, “Okay, let's go.”

“Thank you.” Grey tips his head to her. Being in the same realm with Mila is already calming his nerves a bit. He feels less scattered, but still ready for a fight.

“Don't thank me, just save her,” Silan says with a smile leading them into the castle.

The servants walking the hallways all give Grey a wide berth, some even dipping into open doors to avoid him. His eyes are crazed with the Thirst, and he has to see Mila.

Up two flights of stairs, down a hallway and finally they've arrived outside her room. Silan pauses with her hand on the door, “She was in bad --”

Grey doesn't let her finish, he pushes her aside and goes into the room. His heart sinks to his feet when he sees her.

There's a portly older man standing beside Mila's bed doing a poor job of holding in his emotion. “Who the hell are you?” He barks.

Grey ignores him, focused only on Mila. Her

flesh is decomposing before his eyes. He shakes his head and goes to her side, pushing her beautiful black locks away from her face. "Mila, I'm here."

Mila remains still. The room falls quiet as Grey listens for her heart beat, he hears nothing. "Mila, Mila my love, come back to me." Grey's soul breaking pleas echo off the crystal walls.

An older woman stands from the other side of the bed, "You must be Grey."

Grey nods wiping away the tears blurring his vision.

"I'm so sorry, but it's too late," Keelie says hanging her head.

Grey inhales a deep breath quelling his rage, desire and thirst for blood. He wants to kill every person in this room that's responsible for keeping them apart. He closes his eyes not accepting that she's gone. He channels all of his emotion into her and looks up at Keelie, "It's never too late for love."

Grey's fangs pop out from his gums, and he

slashes his own wrist to drip his blood onto Mila's lips. He gently tugs on her bottom lip to open her mouth. He lifts her other hand to his mouth and begins to drink from her creating an unbreakable circle of their love. The shine from the crystals on the wall gleam brighter. Color and sparkle dance in a magical waltz across the room.

Everyone in the room can feel the energy, a circle of red light forms around Mila and Grey moving around them. Mila's eyes flutter open, she smiles from beneath Grey's wrist and continues drinking. He nods to her, with a flash of lust in his eyes.

Mila's strength returns, her skin is restoring to its previous alabaster state. The life force has come back to her. She threads her fingers from her free hand through his hair pulling him down closer.

"I think perhaps we should give them some privacy," Silan says clearing her throat.

"I will not." Krovo protests firming his stance.

"Krovo," Genevieve barks. "Get out now."

Krovo jumps and notices her for the first time. “Genevieve.”

“Outside, now.” She motions for the door.

They empty out of the room leaving Grey and Mila alone.

Mila swallows one last time. “Grey.” She gasps, “I thought...”

Grey puts his finger to her lips. “I told you I would protect you forever.”

Mila’s being fills with joy and lust. She pulls herself up to him, nibbling on his neck, “I’ve missed you.” She growls.

“I’ve missed you too.” He laughs slightly at the tickle on his neck. “Don’t you think you should get some rest?”

“I don’t need any rest.” Mila plunges her hand down his pants taking his cock into her hands and stroking it lightly. “It seems like you don’t need any rest either.”

Grey lets out a ragged breath in response to her touch, fire shoots through his being. He has to have her, fill her, worship her body like the shrine that it is.

Grey drags his hands across her neck down to the buttons on her shirt. He flicks each button open one by one and lays her gently across the bed, "Are you sure you're feeling okay?" He asks with concern, hoping she says yes.

"I've never felt better," Her eyes are on fire with lust. She unbuttons his shirt raking her fingers across his chiseled chest. "I need you inside me, Grey."

Grey's eyes roll back in his head momentarily at the prospect of feeling the walls of her pussy pulsing around his hard cock. He finishes undressing and pauses a moment to take in all of her beauty. Mila reaches down fondling his erection, urging him closer.

"Patience my love, I want to take in every inch of your body." He says in a low growl.

"And I want every inch of you inside me." She rubs her thumb over his head, spreading the liquid from the tip over him. She brings her thumb to her mouth to taste him. Her mouth explodes with his essence.

Grey lowers himself to her, his lips dancing lightly up her belly to her breasts. Her nipples harden to tight buds that he drags his teeth across sucking one into his mouth while working the other between his finger and thumb.

A whimper gets trapped in Mila's throat, "Grey."

He glances up at her with a devilish grin, "Yes, my sweet?"

She tangles her fingers in his hair pulling his lips to hers. She invites his tongue to play in her mouth, they circle and dance as their breathing mingles in one sweet breath.

Mila gently reaches down and rubs his tip against her clit. Her back arches into the pleasure. Grey lowers himself to her opening, taunting and teasing. He nibbles at her ear, "You want it?"

"God yes!" She groans.

He pushes his cock inside her tight walls, wet and ready for him. He lets out a groan of pleasure, "Mila. You're so fucking tight."

She bites her lower lip and squeezes him tighter

inside him. His eyes roll back in his head before he starts rhythmically pumping inside her. His thrusts careful and slow to feel every part of her swelling around him. "This is what heaven must feel like."

Mila runs her fingers across his chest, playing with the thin sheen of sweat. She wraps her legs around him tighter pulling him into her, deeper, "More." She demands, "Harder."

Grey doesn't comply, he moves himself all the way out of her, teasing at the entrance of her pleasure. She grips her legs tighter pulling him into her. He thrusts into her hard.

A primal moan roots in her throat as she takes all of him in, "Again."

He pulls himself nearly all the way out and thrusts in again and again. His cock spreading her open each time and her sounds of pleasure urging him on more and more.

His arms shake with desire, he's holding back so he can give her more.

He leans up and slides his hands under her ass, lifting her up to him on his knees. She wraps her ankles around his neck and begins again slowly gliding his cock inside her, reaching the sensitive bundle of nerves at the top of her channel.

Mila stiffens and then relaxes into the intensity of the feeling, her breathing becomes more ragged and uneven.

Grey smiles watching her expressions of ecstasy. He massages both of her breasts as he thrusts. Mila's skin is flushed and her pussy swells even more around his steely erection.

He's coming close to the edge and he's taking her with him.

Mila moves her hips in time with his in a beautiful culmination of lust, her whimpers fill the air and she writhes uncontrollably.

Grey takes control of her body, holding her waist, pulling her down to meet the base of his cock. He can feel her walls begin to spasm pushing him over the edge.

He lets out a loud roar as they come in a crescendo of pleasure.

Grey releases her waist dragging his hands up her

smooth skin. Mila unfurls her legs and wraps them around his waist.

He collapses on her, his breathing still ragged, their bodies twitching with the aftershocks of orgasm.

Mila tries to catch her breath, but can't. Grey rolls over to his side, pulling her to his chest. "I can live an eternity like this."

"As can I." She says absently running her fingers across his chest.

He looks deeply into her eyes, "Live a lifetime every night...with me."

"I will." She says smiling.

A Vampire's Thirst

Chapter Twenty-Eight

A light tapping at the door awakens Grey. He gently shakes her, “Mila, someone’s at the door.”

“Tell them to go away.” Mila nuzzles deeper into him.

“Go away,” Grey calls out.

“Mila!” Krovo calls from the other side of the door.

Mila stiffens with fear, and her eyes pop open, “My father.”

“Want me to tell him to go away again?” Grey

asks with a devilish grin.

"I wish." Mila gets up and puts her clothes back on. "You need to get dressed."

Grey blows out a breath and stands from the bed, he goes to her wrapping his arms around her waist, "Are you sure it can't wait?"

"It can't wait, I'm coming in." Krovo barks from the other side of the door.

"One second, Daddy." Mila snaps toward the door.

Grey puts on his pants and sits on the bed. He's not the least bit intimidated by Krovo, he's taking Mila home with him, it doesn't matter what he has to say about it.

Krovo busts in the door, "Mila, this is unacceptable."

Grey positions himself between Krovo and Mila, "She's coming home with me."

"Get out of my way vampire." Krovo tries to move Grey aside unsuccessfully.

"Did you hear me? She's coming home with me." Grey says again in a calm tone.

"She can't, she has responsibilities here. She's betrothed to Elomere and she will be with him." Krovo looks Grey up and down sizing him up.

"She's coming home with me." Grey turns to Mila, "Get your stuff, we're going home."

Mila gathers her things and slides carefully around Krovo.

"Mila, you can't do this." He bellows.

"I am doing this. I'm going to be happy." She says wrapping her arm around Grey's.

"You're just like your mother." Krovo bites.

"I wouldn't know, I wasn't allowed to know her." Mila leads Grey out the door.

"Good luck getting past Cerberus." Krovo cuts a devious smile into his cheek.

Mila stiffens for a moment and looks up at Grey. He gives her hand a squeeze to let her know it will be okay.

"I'm not worried about Cerberus, we'll be able to get home." She starts out the door.

"This is your home, and Cerberus will certainly have fun with your playmate, considering he is dead." Krovo folds his arms across his chest.

"He's not dead, Daddy," Mila pulls her lips to the side. "He got by him before, we'll do it again."

"Of course he was allowed in, but Cerberus will never let a dead man out." Krovo reminds Mila of Cerberus' main function in the Underworld.

Grey shakes his head and reassures Mila that it will be okay, he leans down close to her ear, "He'd have to catch me."

Mila's shoulders relax at remembering Grey's incredible speed. "Yes, he would."

They walk out hand in hand, Silan is in the hallway with a panicked expression. "You need to go fast. He's ordered the army to the portals."

Mila throws her arms around Silan hugging her, "Thank you. I will come back to see you."

"I'll be waiting." Silan bids her farewell with a kind smile.

Mila stops, "Where's my mother?"

"She's waiting for you at the castle gates. Hurry." Silan shoos them down the hallway.

They quickly make their way down the stairs to the castle gates where Genevieve waits. She turns when she hears them coming. "We've got to go. Your father is pissed, and I doubt you're going to be able to leave."

"What about you?" Mila asks her mother with concern. "Don't you worry about me, I won't be going back to New Orleans, I'm going to find a new place to lay low."

"But how will you get past Cerberus?"

A ghost of a smile plays on Genevieve's lips, "Over the past centuries I've made it an art of getting in and out of here undetected."

Mila furrows her brow with question, "What?"

"I was always here, looking in on you. I couldn't go very long without seeing you." Genevieve cups Mila's face in her hands. "I love you, my sweet girl."

"I love you too." Mila's voice is tight with sadness. "Please, find me on the topside."

"I will." She says, "Now go. I want to make sure your father stays put."

Grey looks at Genevieve, "We'll be in New York City. I can protect you there."

"I can protect myself." Genevieve says, "But thank you."

Grey nods and sweeps Mila up into his arms. He runs at full speed past Krovo's armies and to the portal he came through earlier.

He whizzes by Cerberus without incident. Grey places Mila gently on the ground when they come through the portal in New Orleans. He looks around for Clarence or anyone else from The Directive. But the cemetery seems empty.

A soft giggle passes Mila's lips, "Cerberus really wasn't an issue. You're going to have to teach me how to do that."

"Eh, it's a vampire thing." Grey holds her hand leading her toward the car.

Mila swats his chest, "I guess we even each other out then."

"The perfect pair." Grey squeezes her in closer.

"The perfect pair indeed." A menacing voice comes from the darkness.

Mila spins around, "Elomere, I thought you were..."

"No, apparently your little spell wore off," he says stalking toward her.

Grey steps in front of Mila, "Stay back."

"Or what?" Elomere shrugs, "Fairy law states that she's mine."

"She is not property, you can't own her," Grey says in challenge.

"I do own her, and I have no problem killing you to take her." Elomere takes a step closer.

Grey laughs with a sardonic smile. "You think you can kill me?"

"I've killed many, what's one more." Elomere laughs taking another step.

Grey closes the distance between he and Elomere, "I've never killed a blood fairy, but there's a first time for everything."

"Jokes on you, vamp, blood fairies can't die." Elomere launches at Grey.

Grey effortlessly grabs him by the neck holding him up. Elomere disappears from his grasp and reappears next to Mila.

Grey uses his vampire speed to get him away from Mila. Before he can reach them, Elomere has phased out with Mila and reappeared in front of the portal. "I'm taking what's mine." Elomere growls.

Jana steps into the light shining from the portal "You don't belong here, blood fairy." Jana says with a thick accent.

"That's why I'm trying to leave." Elomere's lips are close to Mila's ear.

Grey's blood is boiling, he can only focus on spilling every last drop of Elomere's blood.

Mila struggles to get away from him, but she's unable to move.

Grey calls out to her. "Phase out."

"I can't." She moves her eyes to chain Elomere has wrapped around her wrist.

"You can leave, but you may not take her with you." Jana steps closer.

"Who's going to stop me?" Elomere sneers.

"We will send you back." Clarence comes into view.

Grey takes the opportunity while Elomere is

distracted to rush him. He moves Mila out of the way grabbing the chain and wrapping it around Elomere's neck. Elomere can't recover from Grey's speed, with the chain around his neck he's unable to phase. Grey pulls the chain tighter around Eolomere's.

Clarence takes three steps toward them. "Grey. We need to send him back."

Grey's fangs are protruding from his mouth, he responds with only a growl.

"You can send me back, but I'll keep coming until I get what's rightfully mine." Elomere chokes out the words.

"We will send you back, and you will not return. If we have to destroy every portal, we will." Clarence says calmly. "Grey, you have to let him go. This would not be the best time to anger Magno, he's considering making an exception for you."

Grey hears Clarence's words, but can't quell the need to kill, "He's going to keep coming after her." He grits out trying to control his need for blood.

"You're right, I'll never stop." Elomere goads him on.

"Grey, please let him go." Mila cries out, "You will never win favor with my father if you kill him."

Everyone's voice rings in Grey's head like a cacophony of out of synch drums. He tries to focus only on Mila's heartbeat to calm him, but he can only think of spilling Elomere's blood.

Grey opens his mouth wide sinking his fangs into Elomere's neck. He screeches in pain struggling to get away.

Grey drains nearly every drop from him, stands up and twists his neck until a crunching sound echoes through the cemetery and Elomere goes limp.

"What have you done?" Jana hisses.

"I've ensured that he will not be returning." Grey spits and wipes Elomere's blood from his lips.

"Grey!" Mila runs to him, "Why?"

Grey takes Mila into his arms "To protect you and make sure he never returns."

"The Directive has shown a great deal of patience with you because of the Thirst, but there is no excuse for disobeying a direct order from me." Jana steps menacingly close to Grey.

Grey moves Mila away from Jana shaking his head.

Clarence chimes in with a slow clap, "Well played, Grey."

"You support this action? He disobeyed? Do you really think I can recommend to Magno that she be allowed to stay?" Jana rattles off the series of questions.

"He didn't disobey your order, Jana." Clarence motions down toward Elomere who's beginning to stir.

Jana and Mila look on in confusion, Grey tips his head at Clarence with a knowing look. He releases Mila from his arms and steps over to Elomere. He picks him up by the shirt getting close to his face. "Welcome to the brotherhood, asshole. Good luck with the dog."

Grey tosses Elomere through the portal.

"What just happened?" Mila asks running to Grey.

Clarence eyes Grey with admiration. "He didn't kill him, he made him a vampire."

The revelation crosses Mila's features, "He won't be able to come back. Not without help."

"Exactly, Cerberus will never let him through. It will be centuries before he can develop the speed to get past him." Grey explains.

Jana studies Grey for a moment, "This is your blood fairy?"

"No, this is my Bloodmate." Grey corrects her.

"But a blood fairy nonetheless." She tips her chin down in judgement.

"She's only half blood fairy." Clarence argues.

"That will not change her insatiable appetite for blood. They can't be sustained quietly in this realm." Jana warns.

"But she can." Clarence smiles. "She's with her Bloodmate, his blood will forever sate her thirst."

Jana inhales in deep consideration. "I will speak with Magno." She turns to walk away.

"I can stay?" Mila calls after Jana.

"For now," Jana says without turning around. "I'll be in touch. Or hope that I'm not."

She disappears in the darkness.

"Clarence, you have to speak with Magno, she can't be sent back there." Grey pleads.

"I will speak on your behalf. But you may have to meet with Magno in person." Clarence warns, "And be on your best behavior."

"Of course, we just want to go home." Grey pulls Mila into him.

"I'll do whatever I have to." Mila says in a near panic.

"It's going to be okay." Clarence seems confident that the decision will be in their favor.

"Thank you," Grey says turning back toward the road where he left his car.

"You're welcome, Grey. Please be available for Magno, he'll want you to interview you about your Bloodmate experience."

"I am at Magno's service." Grey leads Mila to the car.

He opens her door for her to get in, and gets in on his side. He leans over and kisses her sweetly on the cheek. "Are you ready to go home?"

"I am." She says crossing the center console to

whisper in his ear, “I want you.”

Grey starts the engine and drives at full speed toward the house.

Prologue

Six months later

Clarence makes his way through the crowded sidewalks of New York to Grey's apartment building in Lower Manhattan. He can hear the sound of laughter coming from inside. He lifts his hand to knock, but the door opens.

"Hello, Clarence." Mila greets him, "Please come in."

Clarence smiles and takes Mila's hand to kiss it. "You're as beautiful as ever."

"Hey, hands off." Grey comes to the door and

shakes Clarence's hand.

"I was just being polite." Clarence winks at Mila.

"Thank you, Clarence." She goes toward the kitchen, "Can I get you a drink?"

"No thank you, I just wanted to check in and see how everything was going." There's something in Clarence's tone that gives Grey pause.

"But this is not just a social visit," Grey asks.

"Yes and no. I've enjoyed getting to know you both, and it's always a pleasure visiting with my favorite new recruit." He smiles and winks at Mila.

"But?" Grey asks.

"I have a message from Magno." Clarence pauses.

"You couldn't send an email?" Grey asks putting his arms protectively around Mila.

"Magno sends his congratulations on your union. But wants to be clear about the upbringing of any offspring." Clarence takes a seat on the couch.

"We don't have any immediate plans for starting our family, so I'm not sure what there is to be clear about," Grey asks taking the seat next to Mila.

"Because there has never been a vampire, blood

fairy offspring before, we don't know what to expect." Clarence pinches the bridge of his nose. "So, we have to keep a close watch on how they progress as they age. We need to be sure that bloodlust doesn't cause any problems."

"I'm sure we're going to be able to teach our children, and make sure they understand humanity and the kindness we must afford all people," Mila says as though it's obvious.

"I know that you will. But the message had to be delivered." Clarence says standing up.

"Was there anything else?" Grey asks.

"No that was it." He starts for the door. "Oh and Mila, there is a training exercise I'd like you to take part in. You're very close to being a full fledged operative for The Directive, there are only a few steps left."

Mila bounces excitedly, "I can't wait, just tell me where and when."

"It will be next week in Germany. I'll email you the details and travel arrangements. I'll see you then." He closes the door behind him.

Mila turns to Grey, riddled with concern, "Do you think there was more to that?"

Grey shakes his head, "No, it was expected." He takes her by the hand and leads her to the balcony. He wraps his arms around her from behind, placing his hands tenderly on her belly, "Our baby will be a first in many ways. We will raise them in a home full of love."

"Grey?" Mila asks wistfully.

"Yes, my love?"

"Be with me forever," She asks.

"Of course, I will be with you through eternity. Because I was meant to." He brushes his lips against her neck sending a fiery rush down her spine.

"So about making babies..." Grey growls in her ear.

Mila relaxes, "I thought you would never ask."

Grey sweeps her into his arms and takes her to the bedroom. "How did I ever get so lucky?"

"We're both lucky to be together." She smiles and buries her nose in his neck nibbling tenderly.

"Forever." Grey says gazing deep into her azure eyes.

"And ever." She smiles back lost in him.

"Forever will never be enough." He breathes the words on her neck tenderly embracing her.

A Note From Bella

Thank you so much for taking the time to read A Vampire's Thirst: Grey. I would be tickled if you would consider leaving a review at your point of purchase or anywhere else you like to review!

If you'd like to stay up to date on news and happenings, you can sign up for my newsletter on my website: bellawrites.com.

You can also find me on Facebook, I'm usually lurking!

Other Works by Bella Roccaforte

The Deadly DreamsSeries

Sketches (Deadly Dreams Book #0)

Fine Lines (Deadly Dreams Book #1)

Vanishing Point (Deadly Dreams Book #2)

Abstraction (Deadly Dreams Book #3)

Darken (Deadly Dreams Book #4)

Bold Strokes (Deadly Dreams Book #5)

Paranormal Transmissions

Season 1: Episode 1 – Push

Season 1: Episode 2 – Manta

Crescent Hunter Series

Moon Crossed (Book 1)

Moon Bound (Book 2)

Wounded Bird Series

Girl on a Swing (Wounded Bird Book 1)

Girl on a Wire (Wounded Bird Book 2)

Girl on the Mend (Wounded Bird Book 3)

A Wolf's Hunger

Saint: A Wolf's Hunger

Mako: A Wolf's Hunger

A Vampire's Thirst

Grey

Stand Alones

Luci: Romance with the Devil's Dauther

What Lurks Within

91012022R00189

Made in the USA
Columbia, SC
14 March 2018